The Proposition

NIGHTS SERIES BOOK SIX

A.M. SALINGER

COPYRIGHT

BOOKS BY A.M. SALINGER

Miles - 7

Urban Fantasy Romance written as
Ava Marie Salinger

Fallen Messengers
Fractured Souls - 1
Spellbound - 2
Edge Lines - 3
Oathbreaker - 4
Harbinger - 5
Crimson Skies - 6
Wicked - Fallen Messengers Short Story Collection

PROLOGUE

I can feel his lips. His kiss. His touch. The weight of his body on me. The lustful look in his eyes. His heat as he enters me. His strength as he takes me. His heavy breaths as he thrusts into my body.

Even in my filthiest fantasies, Wade was never like this. So rough. So demanding. So hungry. He drags me along by brute force, his giant body pinning me down to the bed while he impales me. My field of vision narrows. My reasoning is wrecked. I get muddled.

I want more.

The way Rhys takes me to the hilt, deep in his ass. His moans and his shivers as he rides me. His gasps and the way he trembles when I turn him on his front and do him doggy style. I feel like I'm going out of my mind. I have never been filled with such desire before. The desire to take. To brand.

To tame. To see him submit to me. But also to cherish. To protect. To revere.

This is more than I thought I ever wanted. So much more. And I need it all so badly I can taste him on my tongue. Yearn for him so badly that I wish this moment would never end. One thing I'm certain of.

I will never let him go.

He is my world. And I am his gravity.

CHAPTER ONE

A MUSCLE JUMPED IN RHYS DAMON'S JAW AS HE STRODE across the open plan workspace of the Tokyo branch of Damon & Tucker. He ignored the curious looks of the men and women seated at the neat, uncluttered cubicles lining the ebony floor and stormed inside a large, glass-lined office. He slammed the door shut and glared at the figure on the other side of the sleek desk dominating the stark masculine room while he flicked a switch. The outside world disappeared as the privacy glass changed from clear to frosted.

"Why did you take Misaki off the Osaka project?" Rhys snapped.

Wade Tucker placed his pen down on the file he was working on and leaned back in his leather chair. His expression grew shuttered as he locked gaze with Rhys, his slate blue eyes unreadable.

"She's not fit for it right now."

Rhys inhaled shallowly and counted to five.

Breathe. Just breathe. Don't let him get to you.

"Would you care to explain?" Rhys said between gritted teeth. "We agreed months ago that it was time to give her the lead on one of the new contracts and we did so. We're now six weeks from the deadline. The timing of this couldn't be any worse."

Wade drummed his fingers on the white laminate table, a slight frown darkening his chiseled face. Rhys found his eyes drawn to Wade's large hand and immaculately clipped nails. He wondered if Wade had touched anyone with that very hand the night before. Had dipped his fingers inside a woman's hot mouth and her wet pussy. Had gripped her ass and her hips while he thrust his hard dick repeatedly into her body.

Rhys reigned in on the torrid images flashing across his inner vision and cursed internally.

Now is not the time to indulge in your usual fuck fantasies about this dipshit.

Rhys thinned his lips, leaned against the door, and folded his arms across his chest. "I'm still waiting, Wade."

Wade let out a rueful sigh and ran a hand through his hair. "She's made several mistakes in the past two weeks that would have jeopardized the entire project had one of the other designers on her team not picked up on them."

Surprise jolted through Rhys at Wade's words. It was followed by a surge of irritation. "Why the hell didn't you tell me about this sooner? That doesn't sound like the kind of thing she'd—"

"Because I only managed to pin her down and talk

to her last night," Wade said, his own voice laced with annoyance.

Rhys stilled, his mouth suddenly dry. "Wait...please tell me you didn't sleep with her!"

Shock flared across Wade's face. He scowled and jumped to his feet, his hands flat on the desk.

"What?! *No!* What the hell do you take me for?" he barked.

"An asshole who likes to dip his stick in any wet hole he can find," Rhys said bluntly.

Wade blinked owlishly, his expression so disconcerted Rhys would have laughed had the candid statement he had just made not burned through his very core.

He'd watched Wade bed woman after woman in the sixteen years they had known each other, and it still hurt just as badly as the day he realized he wanted the man who ended up becoming his closest friend and business partner.

Fate is a sick, twisted bitch.

"You're such a fucking contradiction," Wade muttered.

Rhys stiffened under Wade's heated stare. "What do you mean?"

Wade's eyes darkened with a mixture of frustration and amusement.

"You've got that whole suave, sophisticated, butter-wouldn't-melt-in-your-mouth look down to a T," he said, his laser-like blue gaze roaming Rhys from his carefully-styled, dark blonde hair to the polished caps of his Italian loafers, "yet you've got the filthiest mouth of anyone I've ever met."

Rhys ignored the fire licking across his skin where Wade had literally kissed his body with those dangerously mesmerizing eyes of his. He unfolded his arms, pushed away from the door, and tucked his hands in the pockets of his tailor-made trousers as he strolled casually across the office. He stopped opposite Wade and faced him across the desk.

"Of course." Rhys arched an eyebrow arrogantly. "After all, that's why they call *me* The Charmer and *you* The Brute."

Wade's lips twitched at the nicknames that had plagued them since their college days. "I still maintain they should have named us The Joker and The King."

Rhys's shoulders relaxed, the tension that had been with him since that morning slowly abating. "With me in the role of king, obviously," he said tartly.

Wade chuckled, his mouth curving in a lopsided grin that brought out his dimples. Rhys swallowed a groan when he felt his dick stir in response.

Sexy fucker.

Wade's expression gradually sobered. "Misaki's pregnant. And she's thinking about having a termination," he said quietly.

Rhys inhaled sharply, surprise tightening his muscles once more.

Wade sighed. "And no, before you ask, it isn't mine."

Rhys's heart thudded in his chest as he considered Wade. "Who's the father?" he mumbled.

Wade rolled his eyes. "You get one guess."

Rhys's mind raced frantically as he thought of their staff and anyone Misaki had shown interest in of late. From Wade's words, it had to be somebody they both knew.

"Not Reo?" Rhys said. "I know she had a thing for him a while back but he just got engaged, didn't—"

"For one of the smartest guys I know, you sure are dumb sometimes," Wade interrupted, deadpan. "It's Itsuki."

Rhys ignored the insult and frowned. "We haven't got an Its—" He froze as a face swam before his eyes. "*Oh my fucking God*, you mean *that* Itsuki?!"

Wade nodded, his eyes sparkling with mirth at Rhys's stunned expression.

"The *sandwich* guy?!" Rhys spluttered. "That baby-faced kid who looks like he hasn't hit puberty yet? The one who delivers our lunch every day?!"

"Shush, keep your voice down!" Wade said with a frown, eyes darting to the frosted glass separating them from the outer office.

"We both know it's soundproof," Rhys said absent-mindedly. He crossed his arms and leaned his hip against Wade's desk, still startled by Wade's revelation. "Is she serious? About the termination?" he said after a while, chewing his lower lip thoughtfully.

They both knew Misaki was deeply committed to her career at Damon & Tucker. She had been with their Tokyo branch ever since its inception four years ago.

Wade's gaze dropped fleetingly to Rhys's mouth. He sat down slowly.

"I've told her to take some time out and think about

it." He picked up his pen and rolled it between his fingers. "Her head is all over the place right now and, until she makes her decision and comes to terms with it, she won't be able to concentrate fully on work."

"Good move," Rhys murmured. He was still annoyed Wade had kept what had happened from him, but he was also pleased Wade had chosen to address things personally with Misaki first, before hauling her over the coals about her mistakes in front of the entire office. It was one of the reasons they had built such a successful business together and had fiercely loyal employees who rarely jumped ship.

"So, who are you thinking of giving the lead on the project to?" Rhys said curiously.

The pen stilled in Wade's hand. The strangest look flashed in his eyes as he gazed at Rhys.

"I thought you and I could take this one on together." A faint smile curved his sculptured lips. "Like the good old days."

Rhys's stomach plummeted as he stared back at Wade. The last thing he wanted to do with Wade was get back to their "good old days". In fact, he couldn't think of anything worse.

Rhys knew there was no way he could be that close to Wade again without doing something stupid. *Like kiss him. Or jump his bones.*

"It'll please our client. And with the both of us working on it, it won't impact too much on our schedule," Wade continued in a wary tone, as if he were testing the waters.

"What about Gabe?" Rhys said, conscious he was

grinding his teeth. He took a breath and deliberately relaxed his jaw.

"He's got his plate full with the Hawaii project." Wade grimaced. "Besides, I can practically see heart-shaped bubbles above his head whenever I look at him these days. If he wasn't a guy, I'd swear he was pregnant, too. He's positively glowing."

Gabe Anderson, one of their senior and most sought after design consultants, had recently gotten engaged to his boyfriend. Their relationship hadn't been without its trials though, and it was a testament to the two men's commitment to one another that they had come this far in such a short time.

"Well, if anyone could impregnate a guy, I'd say it was Cam Sorvino," Rhys murmured as he thought of the gray-eyed king Gabe had tamed. He smiled faintly when another man's face swam before his eyes, one he knew could also lay claim to that improbable scenario. "Or Joe Cavendish. And you, of course."

Wade startled.

Rhys suppressed a bitter smile at his business partner's expression.

"Don't worry," he drawled in the nonchalant tone he had mastered over the years of his friendship with Wade, "I know you have zero interest in sticking your dick in a man's ass." He pushed away from the desk and started for the door.

"Who's Joe Cavendish?" Wade said.

Surprise flashed through Rhys at Wade's tone. He paused and looked over his shoulder. "A friend."

Lines wrinkled Wade's brow. "You should introduce me, one day."

Rhys blinked. *If I didn't know any better, I'd say that was a hint of jealousy in his voice.* He scoffed at himself internally then. *Yeah, like that would ever happen.*

"I don't think so," Rhys said smoothly.

Wade's frown deepened.

And there it is.

CHAPTER TWO

A SHIVER OF DREAD RAN DOWN RHYS'S SPINE AS HE watched Wade's eyes grow the color of a stormy sky. It was the same expression Wade had worn over the last year at some point or another when they were in the same room together. Or so it seemed to Rhys anyway. He didn't know what had triggered it. This dark, suffocating tension between them.

All Rhys knew was that it was causing a strain in their friendship that could overspill into their business if they weren't careful. He was aware he would have to address it soon. That *they* would have to deal with this, whatever it was.

Yet, the very thought of asking Wade why he seemed to dislike being near him of late made Rhys break out in a cold sweat. Although Rhys desired Wade, *ached* for him in a way that quite frankly scared him, he wasn't ready to let go yet. Wasn't ready to relinquish his bittersweet love for the man who became his roommate at college sixteen years ago. Wasn't ready to bury this sinful secret he had kept hidden deep inside his heart for over a decade.

That the time would come when he would have no choice but to do so was something Rhys was well aware of. But hell if he was going to be the one to end it.

"Let's meet up at eight tomorrow morning and go over the project," Rhys said breezily as he headed for the door once more.

"Why not tonight?" Wade said gruffly.

Rhys ignored Wade's darkening mood and flashed him a bright smile. "I'm afraid I can't. If I'm going to be shackled with that surly attitude of yours for the next six weeks, I need a drink or two."

And preferably someone's dick up my ass or else I'll end up sucking yours before the month's out, whether you like it or not. And I know just the person who'd be willing to oblige me.

Rhys exited Wade's office, smiled at the men and women who glanced his way, and reached for his cell.

WADE SLOWLY UNCURLED HIS FINGERS FROM THE PEN HE was clutching in a death grip. A frustrated sigh left his lips as he stared at the door where Rhys had disappeared. The privacy glass was still frosted, something Wade was grateful for. Or else he would have glared at Rhys as he watched him walk all the way back to his own office. And checked out the way his perfect ass fitted in those tailor-made Italian trousers of his.

Fuck.

Wade dropped the pen on the desk and ran his hands through his hair as he leaned back in his chair. He closed his eyes and sighed.

When did I start thinking that way about him?

Though he'd asked himself that question a hundred times over in the last few months, Wade knew full well what had started this unhealthy obsession he had developed for his close friend and business partner. He could picture it clearly even now, a year after the incident.

It hadn't been Wade's intention to crash at Rhys's place that night. To be fair, Wade hadn't expected Rhys to even *be* at his apartment after he'd said he was going away for the weekend.

Rhys's private life had always been a source of intense fascination for Wade ever since they became college roommates. Though he knew women gravitated to the both of them like moths to flames, Rhys because of his debonair, 60s-movie-star-icon looks and Wade because of his hulking physique, arresting face, and ruthless go-get-it attitude, Rhys had always been secretive when it came to his conquests. And he'd kept it that way since, to the point that Wade often wondered why he was so obsessively discreet.

He stopped wondering the day he saw Rhys jacking off in bed and shouting out Wade's name as he climaxed.

They'd had keys to each other's place ever since they

relocated to Tokyo to grow the Asia branch of their business two years ago. Hell, they had keys to each other's place even when they lived in Chicago.

Crashing at Rhys's apartment was nothing new to Wade, although he tended to do it less often these days. That winter night, Wade knew he'd had too much to drink. Though he could have stayed in the hotel room where he'd bedded that evening's conquest, a model turned actress, he'd made it a habit never to wake up in the same bed where he'd fucked a one-night stand. And since most of his conquests were one-night stands, he practically always slept alone.

Even though he could just as easily have taken a cab to his own apartment, Wade decided to go to Rhys's place since it was closer. He'd stumbled into the immaculate foyer of the multi-million-dollar modern condo in central Tokyo, slipped out of his dress shoes, and had been making his way to the guest quarters when he saw soft light spilling out under the door of Rhys's bedroom at the end of the hall.

Surprise had jolted through Wade then and dampened the effects of the alcohol still coursing through his veins. He'd stood there hesitating for a moment as he wondered whether to let Rhys know he was crashing at his place for the night. That was when he heard it.

A moan.

The sound had frozen Wade's feet to the ground. Heat had flooded his face in the next instant when he realized Rhys had someone with him. Someone he was evidently having sex with. Wade was berating himself for being an ass and had decided to leave Rhys's apartment and go back to his own place when the moan came again.

It was louder. Breathy. Sensual. And most definitely male.

Awareness slammed into Wade with the force of a speeding train. He knew that voice. Had known it for sixteen years.

He moved then, his feet taking him unbidden toward golden light spilling on hardwood floor, his racing pulse sending blood thundering in his ears. As the hairs rose on his arms and his mouth went dry, Wade ignored the internal voice screaming at him that this was a bad idea, that he didn't have the right to do this.

To watch his best friend have sex.

But overwhelming curiosity fueled by alcohol clouded his better judgement and Wade found himself standing in front of Rhys's bedroom in the blink of an eye. The door was slightly ajar. He saw his own hand rise and push it open a few inches as if in a dream.

Wade swallowed as he acknowledged a staggering truth to himself in that split-second before he looked up. He needed to see. Was desperate to see who had elicited such a sound from the refined man he had come to know and respect. A man Wade had never been able to fully figure out, despite over a decade of friendship.

The sight that met Wade's eyes had his breath locking in his throat and his heart stuttering in his chest.

Just like the rest of the apartment, Rhys's bedroom was an elegant mix of grays, blacks, silvers, and whites. Dominating the stylish space to the right and visible through the gap in the doorway was a large, charcoal, modern sleigh bed which Wade knew faced a floor-to-ceiling glass wall overlooking a terrace and the city at the opposite end.

Everything blurred out of focus as Wade stared at the man lying atop the gray sheets. The naked man who was very much on his own and masturbating while he pushed a large, flesh-colored dildo up his ass.

Sweat beaded Rhys's forehead and upper lip as he dug his heels into the mattress and thrust up, his hips undulating in time to his busy hands as he squeezed and rubbed his glistening, engorged cock while driving the lubed love stick between his thighs in and out of his body.

A tortured sob left Rhys's lips as a spasm of pleasure shuddered through him.

The sound traveled down Wade's body and straight to his groin. Wade stared, entranced, as Rhys writhed on the bed and pleasured himself. There was no shame. No guilt that what he was doing was wrong. That watching Rhys in this state was a vile transgression of his friend's privacy. Instead, only one thought filled Wade's mind as Rhys's movements grew more frantic, his voice unrecognizable as he moaned and cursed and groaned out in rising ecstasy.

Rhys Damon was as sexy as fuck.

Rhys suddenly stiffened on the bed. He let go of his cock, grabbed the headboard behind him in a white knuckled-grip, and rammed the dildo into his ass once, twice.

Rhys climaxed on the third violent thrust, his spine arching off the mattress in a deliciously tense curve, his toes flexing in the sheets while pulses of cum jetted out of his flushed dick and struck his golden, sweat-slicked chest and stiff nipples.

Rhys's breath hiccupped in his throat a second before he cried out, his face crumpling as he surrendered to pure pleasure.

"Wade!"

Shock blazed through Wade at the sound of his name on Rhys's lips. It brought him back to life in an instant, jolting him out of the hypnotic daze he'd found himself in. He stepped back from the door, turned, and headed rapidly out of Rhys's apartment, more sober than he had ever been in his entire life.

What Wade had witnessed in that illicit, stolen moment stayed with him throughout the cab ride back to his apartment and in the dark hours of the night that followed, while he lay in his own bed and stared blindly at the ceiling. It stayed with him even after he acknowledged that the hard-on he'd been sporting since he left Rhys's apartment was not going to go away without a cold shower and got up to have one at five in the morning. It stayed with him in the months that followed as he bedded woman after woman, each more stunning than the previous one, in a desperate attempt to erase the memory of what he had seen.

But despite the passage of time and his numerous bed partners, Wade still couldn't forget the arresting image of Rhys's face as he climaxed, his breath catching in his throat, his hips flexing off the bed, his mouth open on Wade's name.

Mixed in with the storm of conflicting emotions that had raged through Wade since that day were two startling realizations.

He hadn't been disgusted by the sight of Rhys pleasuring himself. If anything, it had turned him on like little else had since, and he knew full well he hadn't been thinking of those women when he'd been fucking them this past year.

He was stark, raving mad at Rhys. One, for not admitting to Wade that he was either gay or bisexual. Wade wasn't homophobic in the least and had never done or said anything to indicate otherwise. Both he and Rhys had had gay friends while they were at college and employed a score of openly gay employees. Two, Wade was angry at Rhys for hiding his feelings from him.

It was evident from what Wade had witnessed that Rhys liked him enough to use him as a fuck fantasy. And it had left Wade wondering how long that had been going on for. And the more he wondered, the angrier he got. They had been friends for sixteen years. The fact that Rhys didn't trust Wade enough to admit his own sexuality to him hurt Wade to the core. As for not admitting to his feelings, Wade had begrudgingly had to concede that that wasn't exactly an easy thing to do.

And what the hell would I have done anyway if he'd walked up to me one day and said he wanted me?

It was that thought that had preoccupied Wade the most in the past year and had led him to behave like an ass most times he was in Rhys's presence, something that hadn't escaped their employees' notice. Because deep down inside, Wade sensed the answer he would have given would have surprised both himself and Rhys.

And that, right there, made Wade question everything he thought he knew about himself as a man.

CHAPTER THREE

RHYS SHRUGGED INTO HIS COAT BEFORE TURNING TO THE man walking into the foyer of the restaurant from the direction of the restrooms.

"Ready for that nightcap?" Michael Lynch murmured as he took his jacket from the cloakroom attendant.

Rhys smiled. "Sure."

They stepped out into the cold winter night and headed south toward the Shinjuku main strip. As they strolled through the busy evening crowd, Rhys couldn't help notice the flattering looks the women they passed, and some men, cast at his companion.

A financial lawyer for one of the largest private equity firms in New York, Michael had been relocated to the Tokyo branch of the company eight months ago. They'd met at *Saron*, the most exclusive gay club in town, some three months back and hit it off straight away. It helped that Michael was some six foot three, with thick dark hair and blue eyes, and looked like he could be a distant cousin of Wade's.

It didn't take long for Rhys to discover that they had great chemistry both in and out of the bedroom. Had it not been for the fact that his heart completely and irrevocably belonged to Wade Tucker, Rhys might even have considered the possibility of changing his relationship with the lawyer from sex friends to something more meaningful. Although they'd both made it clear from the get-go that theirs would be a casual association, Rhys knew from Michael's increasingly possessive demeanor that he wouldn't mind getting serious and making things official between them. Rhys couldn't ignore the seed of guilt that had been growing inside him since he'd noticed the change in Michael's behavior.

He looked at Michael as they turned into the inconspicuous side alley where *Saron* was located and wondered not for the first time if he was being a tease and leading the man on.

Well, as long as we're having great sex and no one is getting hurt, I don't mind if we carry on seeing each other.

"What?" Michael said, arching an eyebrow as he noticed Rhys's stare.

"Nothing," Rhys said with a faint smile. "I'm just thinking you look good tonight."

Michael's eyes darkened. He reached out and took Rhys's gloved hand as they approached the suited doorman guarding the steel doors of the club.

"You know better than to say things like that to me,"

Michael said in a thick voice. He raised Rhys's hand and dropped a kiss on his knuckles.

Rhys bit his lower lip and shivered at the sexual heat in Michael's gaze.

Looks like I'm going to get fucked long and hard tonight.

Rhys grinned at that thought. He could think of nothing better to help him forget about Wade and their encounter in his office that morning.

"Mr. Damon, Mr. Lynch," the doorman murmured as he unclipped a rope from a pair of stanchions.

"Kiba," Rhys replied with a nod.

Michael greeted the doorman warmly as the latter opened the door for them. A wave of heat and the sound of jazz music washed over them when they strolled inside the club.

❦

WADE GRITTED HIS TEETH AS HE STARED AT THE TWO men sitting with their thighs touching and their heads tilted toward one another at the polished mahogany bar on the other side of the crowded club. Rhys chuckled at something his companion said and placed his hand on the man's knee. The man covered Rhys's fingers with his own and gripped them lightly.

Wade's entire body tightened where he sat in one of the booths at the back of *Saron*. His knuckles whitened on the glass in his hand. He brought it to his lips and took an angry gulp of his Scotch. The liquid scorched his throat and fanned the fire burning inside him.

Tonight was a night of many firsts for Wade.

It was the first time he'd stalked Rhys to see where his friend and business partner was going to go unwind for the day and have that elusive drink he'd mentioned.

It was the first time he'd been consumed with the intense longing to beat the shit out of a perfect stranger when he'd seen the man Rhys had met at an upscale restaurant in Shinjuku. As he sat in a cafe across the road and watched the pair have dinner through the glass windows of the restaurant, it didn't escape Wade's notice that Rhys's companion looked very much like Wade himself. As that realization sank in, Wade found his indignation turning to fury.

It was also the first time he'd visited a gay club in Tokyo.

When he'd followed Rhys and his companion from the restaurant, Wade hadn't been sure exactly what to expect. He'd told himself he would tail them until their final destination, wherever that may be. The fact that *that* could end up being the stranger's place, or even worse, Rhys's apartment, was a reality Wade told himself he would just have to deal with if it came to that.

Surprise had flashed through him when he'd spotted the club in the dingy alley they'd headed into. It had been rapidly superseded by outrage when he'd seen the asshole Rhys had had dinner with kiss Rhys's hand before they entered the place.

The doorman had hesitated briefly when he'd seen Wade walk up to the club's entrance. One look at the vein throbbing in Wade's temple and a quick scan of his tailored suit and dress shoes was all it took for the man to unclip the rope guarding access to the place.

The interior of *Saron* had been Wade's fourth surprise of the night. As he'd studied the unique decor of the club, Wade's anger had reached boiling point. He could see Rhys's touch all over the place and knew instinctively his business partner had kept this little side endeavor a secret from him too.

Wade wondered how many more of Rhys's secrets he would uncover before this night was over.

He'd just glanced at his watch when movement to the right caught his gaze. A man was strolling down the steps of the club. At six foot three, with dark hair and a stubbled jaw, he was dressed in a casual suit and carried himself with a bearing that oozed confidence and sex appeal. The crowd parted ahead of him, the club patrons calling out greetings as he passed them, many following him with longing gazes.

The man headed behind the bar, dropped a kiss on the lips of the blond bartender who'd served Rhys and his companion, and greeted Rhys with a warm smile.

Wade scowled. *And who's this fucker?*

Rhys said something to the newcomer. The man's smile widened, amusement sparkling in his eyes as he glanced from Rhys to Rhys's companion. The blond bartender frowned at Rhys. Rhys laughed and took a sip from his tumbler.

Rhys's companion reached up suddenly and ran his thumb over Rhys's glistening lower lip.

Wade straightened in his seat, his back rigid.

Rhys's eyes grew hooded as he gazed at his

companion. He finished his drink, said something in the man's ear, and climbed off the barstool. Wade tracked Rhys with a heated stare as the latter headed for the back of the club.

"Is this seat taken?" someone murmured.

Wade looked at the man standing next to his booth. Though he'd been aware of the men in the club checking him out as if he were a piece of prime meat, this guy was the first one who'd actually had the nerve to speak to him.

"It is," Wade said curtly.

The man studied the obviously empty space beside Wade for a beat before nodding and strolling off into the crowd.

Wade's gaze shifted back to the bar. His stomach dropped when he saw that Rhys's companion was also missing. He scanned the club with narrowed eyes and caught sight of the man just as the latter disappeared through a door at the back.

CHAPTER FOUR

Rhys glanced in the mirror at the sound of the restroom door opening. He finished drying his hands and turned to smile at the man strolling toward him.

"What, you couldn't wait for me to get—"

The rest of Rhys's words were swallowed by Michael's lips as he grabbed Rhys's chin and crushed their mouths together. Rhys gasped when Michael gripped his hips and lifted him up onto the edge of the black marble countertop before settling between his thighs. Ever the opportunist, Michael slipped his tongue inside Rhys's mouth and started frenching him in earnest.

Rhys welcomed the rough mating for a couple of heartbeats before pushing at Michael's chest and chuckling against his lips.

"Whoa, slow down. What's the rush?" He arched an eyebrow at Michael's burning stare and cocked his head toward the door. "Besides, unless you're planning on putting on a show, we should do this back at your place."

Michael nipped at Rhys's lower lip with his teeth. "I suddenly feel very horny," he said huskily. "Blame it on someone who complimented me on my looks earlier tonight. I put the 'Cleaning in progress' sign in front of the door, so no one should disturb us."

Rhys's gaze dropped to the obvious bulge straining the front of Michael's pants. He ran a finger down it and grinned when Michael shuddered and cursed.

"You mean, little ole me is responsible for putting you in this, how should I put it, *inflamed* state?" he murmured.

"You know very well you are," Michael groaned. He pulled Rhys against him and swooped down to take his mouth in a hot kiss.

Rhys grabbed Michael's shoulders, locked his legs around Michael's thighs, and surrendered to the moment, his own cock hardening behind his zipper.

He was starting to think having a quickie in the restroom was a damn perfect way to begin the fuck fest that would be the rest of the night when someone wrenched Michael away violently and sent him slamming backward into a stall door to Rhys's left.

WADE'S BREATHS LEFT HIS LIPS IN HARSH, SHUDDERING pants as he glared at the two men staring at him across the club's restroom, their expressions so shocked it would have been comical under any other circumstance.

Somewhere at the back of his mind, Wade knew he was acting irrationally. But when he'd walked through that door and seen Rhys wrapped around the man he'd been flirting with all night like a rose coiled on a vine and kissing him passionately, something inside him had finally snapped.

"Wade?" Rhys said hoarsely. He blinked, his dilated pupils constricting as he seemed to finally grasp what had just happened. The color drained from his face. "What—," he swallowed convulsively, knuckles whitening where he gripped the edge of the marble countertop, "what are you—"

"*Hey, asshole!* What the fuck do you think you're doing?!" roared Rhys's companion. He straightened from the door he'd crashed into and charged across the room.

Wade cast him a deadly glare and pressed his hand against the man's chest as the latter stopped next to him.

"Don't," Wade said in a savage voice even he didn't recognize, his gaze swinging around to lock on Rhys's wild-eyed stare once more.

The man froze. He looked slowly between Wade and Rhys, evidently sensing the undercurrent of pure tension running between the two men.

"Rhys, who is this guy?" he said with a scowl.

Rhys startled and blinked. He broke eye contact with Wade and gazed blindly at the man he'd been kissing barely a minute ago.

"He's—he's my—," Rhys mumbled.

"I'm his partner," Wade said icily.

Rhys's companion inhaled sharply, shock flaring across his face once more.

Rhys stiffened. He narrowed his eyes at Wade, some of his color returning as he finally came out of the shocked daze he'd been in.

"Business partner," Rhys said, his voice hardening. He dropped down from the counter and looked at his companion. "I'm sorry Michael, but can we call it a night? I need to talk to Wade." He ran a hand through his hair and gave the man an apologetic half-smile.

Wade didn't miss the fact that the smile didn't quite reach Rhys's pale and very much angry eyes. Quite frankly, Wade didn't care. As long as Rhys sent the man he'd been intending to spend the night with packing, Wade was prepared to deal with Rhys in any state he found him in. He glanced down and felt his dick throb.

Even one where he has a raging hard-on.

❦

RHYS OPENED THE DOOR OF HIS CONDO AND FELT A draft of air on the back of his neck as Wade came in behind him. Rhys shrugged out of his coat, dropped it on a hook on the stand in the foyer, and turned to glare at the hulking figure standing silently a few feet from him.

Rhys folded his arms across his chest. "Well? What do you have to say for yourself?" he said coldly.

Wade took his coat off, threw it on the stand, and

stormed past Rhys, his gorgeous face set in grim lines. Rhys ground his teeth together and turned to follow him into the lounge. Wade strode to the bar next to the floor-to-ceiling glass wall overlooking the terrace that wrapped around the condo, poured himself a Scotch, and downed it.

Despite the maelstrom of emotions that had been roaring through Rhys since the moment he'd seen Wade in *Saron's* restroom, he couldn't help but admire the way Wade's Adam's apple bobbed as he swallowed angrily.

Why couldn't he just look like the Hunchback of Notre Dame for one goddamn second?

Rhys still couldn't believe Wade had been there tonight. That Wade had seen him kissing Michael. That Wade had pulled Michael off him as if he had prior claim to Rhys himself, a claim Wade openly asserted when he said he was Rhys's partner.

Rhys closed his eyes briefly before tugging at his necktie.

Well, that cat is well and truly out of the bag now. He knows I'm gay.

On the tail end of that thought came an unsettling realization.

And he doesn't seem in the least bit bothered by it.

Not that Rhys thought for one minute Wade would act like a homophobe. It was just that admitting his sexuality to him would have put Wade a step closer to one day realizing that Rhys had feelings for him.

Another wave of guilt washed over Rhys when he recalled Michael's expression while he'd been trying to convince the lawyer that he was going to be okay. As Michael finally left the club's restroom, Rhys couldn't miss the hurt look in his eyes when he'd cast a final glance at Wade. It had to be obvious to Michael that he bore a striking resemblance to the man who had barged in on the two of them and who stood glaring at the lawyer as if he were a child killer.

A heavy silence had fallen between Rhys and Wade after the door swung close behind Michael. Rhys had hesitated before heading for the exit. A hand had closed around his wrist in an iron grip before he could reach it, halting him in his tracks.

"Where are you going?" Wade said silkily.

Rhys's heart pounded erratically as he looked from where Wade's fingers lay against his skin, to the stormy blue eyes boring into him. He knew Wade could feel his racing pulse where he was touching him.

"Back to my apartment," Rhys said in as stony a voice as he could muster.

"I'm coming with you," Wade said gruffly.

"I didn't expect anything less," Rhys retorted.

To Rhys's shock, Wade had kept a firm grip on his hand as they headed back into the club, as if he were afraid Rhys would run off and disappear into the night. And he didn't let go even after they got in a cab and headed over to Rhys's place. In fact, it wasn't until they entered the lift that would take them up to the apartment that Wade finally relinquished his deadly hold on Rhys's arm, the strained hush between them since they'd left the club's restroom still in place.

Wade finished his drink, wiped his lips with the back of his hand, and turned to stare at Rhys.

"Why did you never tell me you were gay?"

Rhys swallowed a sigh. *Here we go.* "Because it's none of your business."

A muscle jumped in Wade's cheek. "I'm your best friend."

Rhys shrugged. "So? That doesn't give you the right to know about my sex life."

"It does when I'm the subject of your fuck fantasies!" Wade roared.

CHAPTER FIVE

WADE CURSED HIMSELF INTERNALLY AS HE WATCHED Rhys turn to stone.

Wade knew he was hurting Rhys with his overbearing manner and his cruel words. Knew he had been a complete asshole for barging in on Rhys and his lover and forcing Rhys to send the other man away. Knew he had no right to be here right now, interrogating Rhys as if he were a criminal.

Except I have. Since the day I realized he wanted me. He owes me an explanation. And it's about time I got one.

"What did you just say?" Rhys whispered, his face ashen.

Wade pushed away from the bar and stepped toward Rhys.

Rhys unfroze and stepped back.

Wade stopped then, his heart thumping in his chest, conscious he needed to keep his distance for the next precious few moments. He could see Rhys slowly unravelling before him, the carefully guarded, nonchalant mask he normally sported slipping from his beautiful face, exposing such raw emotion it took all of Wade's willpower not to walk over and take him in his arms.

"Rhys," Wade breathed.

Rhys shuddered at the sound of his name and closed his eyes, as if he couldn't bear to look at Wade.

"I saw you," Wade admitted in a quiet voice in the frozen hush. "A year ago. I came here one night to crash at your place."

It was several long seconds before Rhys took a ragged breath and finally spoke. "What—," he swallowed, opened his eyes, and licked his lips, "what did you see?"

"You. In bed. You were jacking off." Wade hesitated before meeting Rhys's stunned gaze head on. "You called out my name when you came."

Rhys's hands slowly fisted by his sides.

Pain squeezed Wade's heart as he watched Rhys's eyes darken with a tumult of emotions. Disbelief. Shame. And an agony so deep it seemed it would tear the man he was looking at apart.

Rhys gripped his head with his hands and twisted on his heels, turning his back on Wade.

"This isn't happening. This isn't fucking happening," Rhys said hoarsely, fingers curling in his hair.

Alarm flashed through Wade when he saw the shivers racking Rhys's body. He closed the distance between them and touched Rhys's shoulder.

"Hey, calm down. I didn't—"

RHYS FROZE AT WADE'S TOUCH.

"*Don't!*" he barked.

He felt Wade startle behind him. Wade slowly removed his hand from Rhys's shoulder.

"Just…don't," Rhys whispered, his voice breaking as despair threatened to drown him.

Never in a million years could Rhys have imagined that Wade already knew about his sick, sinful longing for him. Had known for a year, it seemed.

But he never said any—

Rhys's eyes widened.

No. He didn't say anything. But he showed me how he felt. Every time he was in the same room with me, he showed me. With his body. With his words. With his eyes.

Nausea churned Rhys's stomach as he finally realized the reason behind the growing friction between Wade and him in the last twelve months. It had obviously started after Wade witnessed him masturbating and crying out his name as he reached his orgasm. And what Wade had seen had obviously pissed him off big time.

Rhys lowered his trembling hands to his sides, blood pounding dully in his ears and casting red pulses across his vision while he stared blindly at the floor.

So, this is it. This is how it ends.

Even though Rhys's heart screamed that he wasn't ready yet, wasn't even anywhere near willing to let go of his forbidden love, he knew there would be no escape from what was unfolding between Wade and him right now. He inhaled shallowly and finally turned to face Wade. They studied each other for a timeless moment, slate-blue eyes locked on baby blue, each watching, waiting, the silence between them so taut a whisper would shatter it.

Wade took a step toward Rhys.

This time, Rhys stood his ground. He curled his fingers into fists and tilted his chin to look up at Wade when the latter stopped a foot opposite him.

"How long?" Wade said stiffly, his gaze roaming Rhys's face, as if he were seeing him for the very first time.

Rhys cleared his throat, not sure why he suddenly felt so nervous under Wade's laser-like stare.

Well, actually, no. I'm on edge because I'm waiting for him to punch my lights out.

"How long what?" Rhys croaked.

Wade's gaze dropped lower. "How long have you been fantasizing about me?"

Is he staring at my mouth?

Rhys swallowed and wet his lips. Wade's pupils dilated.

Yup, he's definitely staring at my mouth.

Rhys's racing heart skittered all over the place as Wade continued staring at his lips.

What the fuck is going on here? Why is he looking at me like that?

"I'm waiting, Rhys," Wade said silkily.

Oh hell!

The tension coiling through Rhys exploded in a

flurry of charged words as he finally threw caution to the winds.

"You mean how long have I wanted you? Twelve years!" Rhys snapped. "How long have I thought that your dick would be the best thing I could ever suck on? About the same length of time. And you fucking me? I mean, *really* fucking me, as in *your* dick in *my* ass, well, I guess it's hardly going to come as a surprise when I say twelve—"

"You ever thought of sticking it in me?" Wade interrupted.

Rhys opened and closed his mouth soundlessly, his train of thought completely derailed by Wade's question and the curious look in his eyes.

"What?!" Rhys finally spluttered. "*No!* I'm more catcher than pitcher. Besides, why the hell are you even—"

"What about the dildo?" Wade said.

Rhys rocked back on his heels and blinked.

Wade lifted a hand and cradled Rhys's chin in his palm, holding him in place. "What about the dildo, Rhys?" he repeated thickly.

Oh God. This is Hell, isn't it? I'm in Hell. Sometime tonight, I had an accident and now I'm in purgatory, condemned to being tortured by this devil who looks like Wade.

A shiver raced down Rhys's spine as his skin absorbed Wade's touch and his body unconsciously angled into the intoxicating heat radiating off the powerful male frame towering over him. He'd never stood this close to Wade before, toe to toe and nose practically to nose.

Fuck, he smells good.

"I saw it," Wade said. He leaned down and brought his lips to Rhys's left ear. "You were using it when you were masturbating. It was big and long and thick. And you looked like you were really enjoying driving it up your ass. In fact, you came just from the dildo."

Rhys gasped, his dick coming to life in one, rock-hard second at the wicked feel of Wade's breath on his skin and the filthy words rolling off his tongue.

Wade's heart thrummed against his ribs when he felt a shudder run through Rhys.

Twelve years. Twelve fucking years.

Shock reverberated through Wade at Rhys's stormy admission. He couldn't believe he'd been blind for so long. Couldn't believe he'd been unable to read his best friend for that length of time.

Wade thought of all the women he'd bedded during those years, many of whom he'd gone off with while in Rhys's company. He winced internally as he studied Rhys's bewildered expression.

Poor baby. He must have been through hell and back.

It was clear to Wade that what he was doing and saying was shocking the hell out of Rhys. He'd guessed from Rhys's initial reaction a couple of minutes ago that the latter had probably expected to be told off, or worse, punched for admitting to lusting after Wade.

As for Wade, he finally knew the answer to the

question that had haunted him for the last year. Deep down inside, he'd probably always known. It had taken seeing Rhys with another man tonight for it to become clear. And it was hearing Rhys's reluctant confession just now that had crystallized it into an irrevocable conviction.

And hell if that didn't make Wade hard.

CHAPTER SIX

He's lost his fucking mind. There's no other explanation for what's happening right now. He hit his head and he's lost his mind.

Rhys stared wildly at Wade as the latter drew his head back slightly, his fingers still holding Rhys's chin captive.

I mean, does he even realize how close I am to losing my shit right now? If he keeps touching me like this, I'm going to come in my pants like a fucking teena—

That was when Wade leaned down and pressed his lips to Rhys's. Rhys gasped, his heart literally skipping a beat. His eyes widened as he gazed into Wade's focused stare while the latter curiously molded their lips together.

Rhys pushed Wade away and stepped out of his reach, his breaths coming in harsh, panicked pants, his body trembling so hard he thought his knees would give out beneath him.

He kissed me! He—

"*What the fuck are you doing?!*" Rhys roared. "You hate me! That's why you've been acting like such an asshole the whole of this year, so why the hell are you touching me and kiss—"

Wade frowned. "I don't hate you."

Rhys froze. He blinked owlishly at Wade. "What?" he mumbled after a stunned moment. "Then, why—"

"Oh, that was just me being angry with you," Wade said dismissively, as if the hell he'd put Rhys through in the past twelve months was water under the bridge.

Rhys scowled. *This asshole!*

"Okay, so you don't hate me, but you're angry with me," he said between gritted teeth, trying his best to ignore his aching cock. "It still doesn't explain why you're acting like you suddenly started batting for the other team or why—"

"I think you're misunderstanding something here, so let me make things crystal clear," Wade said quietly. "I'm not angry with you for wanting me. I'm angry with you because you *hid* it from me. And this isn't about me suddenly finding out I'm gay either."

A lightheaded feeling swept over Rhys as he stared at Wade.

Does the dumb bastard even know what he's saying right now? If I'm hearing him right, he means—

Rhys lifted his chin defiantly at Wade, his nails biting into his palms as he phrased the question he so very much wanted to ask.

"So what? Are you saying if I'd told you I wanted you all those years ago, you would have responded in kind? That you would have welcomed my advances despite the fact that I'm a man—"

"I don't know about years ago," Wade interrupted. "But twelve months ago? Six months ago? Hell, six minutes ago?" Wade stormed across the floor, took Rhys's face in his hands, and stared heatedly into his eyes. "It doesn't matter that you're a man. You're you. My best friend. The person I'm closest to in the entire world. The person I respect more than myself." A mocking laugh left Wade's lips then. He closed his eyes briefly before boring into Rhys's shocked stare once more. "The person who always kept part of himself hidden from me, for all those years. My very own enigma. And now I know why. You wanted me. All this time, you wanted *me*."

Fire swept through Rhys's entire body as Wade rubbed a thumb across his mouth. Rhys licked his lips unconsciously and nearly groaned when the tip of his tongue touched the pad of Wade's finger. Wade's pupils dilated before his gaze grew hooded.

"So, no, it doesn't matter that you've got a dick and balls instead of a pussy, Rhys," Wade continued in a gravelly voice that shot straight down Rhys's spine and made his hole twitch. "You know what went through my mind when I saw you naked in your bed that one time? I thought you were sexy as fuck. And the sight and sound of you climaxing that night? God, it left me with such a hard-on I took several cold showers before my dick calmed down."

With that, Wade swooped down and took Rhys's mouth in a scorching kiss.

❦

Soft. That was Wade's immediate impression of their first proper kiss. *His lips are soft. And just a bit chapped from chewing them so damn much.*

Wade's fingers flexed on Rhys's skin. He steered Rhys backward to the closest wall and crowded him in before angling his head to get better access to Rhys's lips.

A breathy sound left Rhys when Wade aligned their bodies together and pressed him into the wall. To Wade, it sounded very much like the white flag of surrender.

Finally.

He started his attack in earnest, probing Rhys's lips with his tongue, seeking entrance, dying to get his first full taste of the enigmatic man who had bewitched him body and soul.

❦

Oh God. Pinch me. I can't believe this is really happen—

Rhys inhaled raggedly as Wade's tongue swept past his lips and invaded his mouth. The scandalous words Wade had just spoken faded from his mind like mist in sunlight as he soaked in the sensation of their first kiss.

Rhys shivered and clutched at Wade's shoulders when Wade's tongue clashed deliciously with his.

Fuck. Me.

Rhys was an experienced man. He'd kissed plenty of

guys, and some women, in his lifetime and knew full well how to tempt and tease someone with his lips and tongue.

Right now, he felt about as accomplished as a blushing virgin on her wedding night. Because Wade Tucker was a fucking master at kissing. And if he kept on doing what he was doing with his wicked mouth and his filthy tongue, Rhys knew he would embarrass himself and come apart in Wade's arms in a matter of seconds.

WADE TASTED SCOTCH AND MINT AND SOMETHING ELSE as he delved deep into Rhys's mouth. It took his brain a moment to process what it was. A groan rumbled up his throat when he registered the sinful truth.

It was the flavor of Rhys himself. His quintessential essence. And darn if it wasn't as addictive as the finest elixir.

Wade wrapped his tongue around Rhys's in an intimate caress, seeking more of the intoxicating flavor. Rhys moaned and shuddered against him, his skin burning up in Wade's hands.

Something else was burning up farther south.

Fire licked Wade's dick when he felt Rhys's erection probe his left thigh. He flexed his hips and stifled a grin when Rhys trembled in his arms. Wade lined up his own erection with Rhys's, dipped his knees, and rolled his hips back up in a slow, sensual grind that had their cocks rubbing together.

Rhys wrenched his mouth from Wade's and dropped his head back against the wall. "*Fuck!*"

Wade repeated the move before lowering his head and kissing Rhys's exposed throat. He swallowed a grunt of need. *Shit, his skin tastes the same as his mouth.* Wade wondered if Rhys tasted the same everywhere. That thought had his dick doing press-ups behind his zipper. He couldn't wait to find out.

Wade sucked and nibbled on Rhys's neck as he continued rubbing their crotches together. "Does that feel good?"

Rhys grabbed the back of Wade's head, yanked him up until he could stare him in the eye, gave him a wild are-you-fucking-kidding look, and pounced on his mouth like a ravenous man.

Wade chuckled as he welcomed Rhys's passionate kiss. He slipped his hands down Rhys's back and felt him stiffen when he cupped his butt. Wade nipped at Rhys's tongue and was rewarded with a throaty groan as Rhys lost himself in the moment once more. Wade curled his fingers into Rhys's delectably firm ass and held him steady as he continued grinding their bodies and cocks together.

Rhys's breaths left his nose in short, sharp pants, his shudders and moans growing more untamed as he neared his orgasm.

Wade bit back a growl, filled with a sudden, insane need.

I want to see. I want to see his face when he comes.

Wade pulled back from their kiss, brought one hand to Rhys's nape and fixed him in place while he flexed and rolled his hips, kneading his rock-hard dick against Rhys's over and over again. His breath caught when he saw Rhys's face.

Passion had darkened Rhys's eyes to indigo. His cheeks were flushed and his lips red and swollen from their kiss.

So hot. I want to see it all. All the wicked, sinful sides of him I don't know.

Rhys groaned and leaned into Wade, seeking his lips.

Wade shook his head and leveled a burning stare at him.

"What?" Rhys panted, confused.

Wade glanced down to where their cocks were rubbing before looking into Rhys's dazed eyes. "Show me. Come for me."

Rhys's pupils dilated, shock flaring in their depths.

Wade yanked Rhys's butt forward until there wasn't a sliver of space left between their groins as he continued their titillating bump and grind.

Rhys resisted and tried to push Wade away.

Wade dipped his head and bit down on Rhys's lower lip. He tugged on it with his teeth before sucking it between his own lips.

Rhys went rigid against him.

"Come for me, Rhys," Wade ordered gruffly. He thrust his cock hard against Rhys's.

Rhys's breath locked in his throat. His fingers dug into Wade's shoulders as he rose on his toes. Then, he came, loudly, spectacularly, his hips jerking erratically against Wade's while the most filthily arousing cries Wade had ever heard left his lips.

In that moment, Wade knew that they had just crossed a line from which there would be no coming back. Because there was no way in hell he could just be friends with Rhys again. Not after feeling Rhys and tasting him like this. And not after seeing Rhys come apart from his touch.

Rhys Damon was mesmerizing.

And Wade was completely and utterly captivated.

CHAPTER SEVEN

Rhys moved his fingers on the track pad. Schematics scrolled across the dual display monitors on the wall at the end of the room. He picked up a pen, made a note on the writing pad next to him, and sighed before looking up at the man staring at him heatedly from the other side of the table.

"Are you even concentrating on what we're supposed to be doing right now?" Rhys asked Wade testily.

Wade grinned. "Nope."

It was eight fifteen in the morning. They were in one of the conference rooms at Damon & Tucker, where they were going over the details of the Osaka project. Or meant to be, anyway. After the earth-shattering events of the previous night, Rhys was surprised Wade had turned up for their meeting this morning.

Rhys hadn't known how to act or what to expect

when he'd finished climaxing in Wade's arms like a sixteen-year old boy getting his first hand job. For one frozen moment, he'd even wondered if it was all a dream, one of the countless night time fantasies he'd had about Wade since he started lusting after him. But as he'd stood there trembling and breathless in Wade's arms, Wade had tipped Rhys's chin up with a finger and delivered one of the sweetest kisses Rhys had ever been given.

"I think that's plenty enough for tonight," Wade had murmured against Rhys's mouth while the latter blinked drowsily at him. "I'm gonna leave while I can still walk out of here."

Rhys flushed when he registered Wade's erection digging into his hip. "I—"

Wade pressed his finger against Rhys's lips, hushing him. "No. When we do this, and we *will* do this, I want to take my time and savor every single second." A wicked smile curved his lips when Rhys released a ragged breath. "Preferably in bed, with the both of us naked." His smile faded. "And not when you've been touched by another man."

Rhys shivered at the possessive look dawning in Wade's eyes.

"You're gonna dump him, right?" Wade said.

Rhys stared at him dazedly. He'd forgotten all about Michael.

Wade frowned. He leaned down and nipped at Rhys's right ear lobe with his teeth. "Rhys?" he hissed threateningly.

Rhys groaned, his dick twitching again at the feel of Wade's breath and lips on his skin. "Yes! I—I'll talk to Michael."

"You better do more than just talk to him," Wade said with an arrogance that stole Rhys's breath away. "You're not gonna be seeing anyone else from now on."

Rhys narrowed his eyes as he started coming down from the incredible high Wade had just delivered with his body.

"Oh, really?"

"You'd better believe it, hot shot," Wade said gruffly. "I don't share. *Especially* not you."

And with that outrageous comeback, Wade had exited the apartment, leaving Rhys propped against the wall on shaky legs. How Rhys had managed to sleep a single wink that night, he didn't know. He'd woken up at the shrill sound of his alarm and laid there staring at the ceiling for long minutes while he recalled all the deliciously filthy things that had happened between them mere hours before. Still, an uneasy feeling had overshadowed Rhys's recollections as he climbed out of bed and got ready for work.

There were still many questions he needed to ask Wade.

"Misaki's team is coming," Rhys glanced at his watch presently, "in fifteen minutes, so get your mind out of the gutter and start focusing."

Wade linked his hands behind his head and swiveled in his chair. "Oh, I'm focusing all right," he drawled, his hot gaze dropping to Rhys's mouth.

Rhys frowned. *This asshole.*

"In fact, you know what I'm thinking about right now, Rhys?" Wade leaned forward, his tone conspiratorial.

"What?" Rhys mumbled, unable to tear his gaze from the indecent sparkle in Wade's eyes.

"Buns," Wade stated salaciously.

Rhys's eyes rounded. "*What?!*" he spluttered.

"Your ass," Wade elaborated. He opened his hands in front of him and moved them as if he were weighing something. "It fitted my hands just so. And it was—," his fingers flexed, "—firm. Resilient. Pert. In fact, your butt is goddamn perfect."

Rhys propped his elbows on the table and dropped his face in his hands, his ears flaming. "I can't believe we're having this conversation right now," he groaned.

"What?" Wade said.

Rhys wasn't fooled by Wade's innocent tone. "You're really enjoying this, aren't you?" he said, scowling at Wade between his fingers.

"You mean, teasing you?" Wade grinned. "Call it payback. You owe me for the permanent hard-on I've had this year."

Rhys's dick twitched behind his zipper.

"How many?" he asked hoarsely.

Wade looked puzzled. "How many what?"

"How many cold showers did you have last night, after you left my place?" Rhys said, his pulse racing.

Wade smirked. It was a dirty, filthy smile.

"Oh, I had one, very long shower. But it wasn't cold." Wade leaned forward again. "It was hot. As hot as my dick when I jacked off twice to the memory of you climaxing in my arms."

Rhys's breath faltered for dizzying seconds as he pictured Wade standing under the open, waterfall shower in his en suite bathroom, one hand fisted against the black slate wall while he worked his hard cock with the other.

"And Rhys?" Wade said, his deep, rough voice cutting through Rhys's fevered imagination.

"Yeah?" Rhys whispered, enthralled by the hypnotic light darkening Wade's eyes to a gunmetal blue.

"I'm still hard."

Rhys swallowed a groan. *I'm going to die. I'm going to have a heart attack, right here, right now, with a permanent boner on display.*

"Just so you know, I'm coming over tonight," Wade added thickly.

When the conference room door opened and the team working on the Osaka project piled in, Rhys wasn't sure whether to be upset or grateful for the distraction.

※

WADE ADJUSTED HIS PANTS OVER HIS CROTCH BEFORE ringing the buzzer of Rhys's apartment. Although he had the key to the place, tonight felt…special. Wade knew he'd invaded Rhys's privacy yesterday by stalking him and forcing him to admit to his feelings for Wade, before pouncing on him like a starving man. He sensed he needed to give Rhys some breathing space.

Just enough for him to regain his composure, but not enough for him to bolt.

Because something told Wade that Rhys was thinking of making a break for it. Call it a hunter's instinct.

The door opened, revealing Rhys still dressed in his tailored work suit. He'd taken his jacket off and loosened his tie slightly.

He arched an eyebrow at Wade. "What happened to your key?"

Wade swallowed, his palms suddenly sweaty.

Shit. Why am I so nervous?

"Wade?" Rhys said with a small frown.

"What?" Wade mumbled.

A strange look came over Rhys's face then. Wade's heart sank as he registered the emotions flashing in Rhys's blue eyes. They were part bitterness and part resignation.

"Look, I'll understand if you're having cold feet," Rhys said quietly. "We can pretend last night never happened and go back to how things—"

This jolted Wade out of his stupor. "Hell no!" he snapped.

Rhys startled and backed up as Wade stormed across the threshold of the apartment and slammed the door shut. Wade closed the distance between them and took Rhys's face in his hands before fusing their lips together.

Fuck breathing space. He's running away right before my eyes!

Rhys gasped and stiffened, his hands rising to lock around Wade's wrists.

Wade slipped his tongue between Rhys's lips and delved into the hot depths of his mouth. A shudder raced down his spine as he got his first taste of Rhys for that day.

Ah. Heaven.

CHAPTER EIGHT

Rhys's heart raced wildly as he lost himself in the torrid kiss, the fear that had been with him the whole day melting into nothingness. Despite Wade's teasing that morning and the sexual tension that had thrummed between them since, Rhys was convinced Wade would regret what had happened between them. Whether it was today, tomorrow, or the day after, Rhys knew the time would come when Wade would wake up and realize he'd made a dreadful mistake.

It was as inevitable as the tides. Besides, life wasn't this straightforward.

No gay man could expect that the straight friend he'd been lusting after for over a decade would suddenly turn around one day and tell him he wanted him back. Still, Rhys couldn't help fantasize about what it would be like to sleep with Wade. And he was curious to find out just how far Wade could go with him, even if it would only lead to heartache.

So when Wade pushed Rhys all the way through the

apartment, into the lounge, and onto a large, black suede couch, Rhys went with the flow.

Wade could feel his dick doing push-ups behind his zipper as he crowded Rhys on the couch. He pushed Rhys onto his back and pinned Rhys's wrists above his head with his hands before aligning their crotches and flexing his hips. A throaty moan rumbled out of Rhys. He arched up into Wade, his erection pushing against Wade's cock. His tongue lashed hungrily against Wade's.

More. I want more.

Wade reached down with one hand and hurriedly unbuckled Rhys's pants, need pulsing through him and rendering his movements jerky. Rhys stiffened under him and wrenched his mouth free from their kiss, his eyes slamming open. Wade's heart constricted at the gut-wrenching desire and fear he could read in the blue depths.

He leaned down and bumped his nose against Rhys's.

"It's okay," Wade whispered. "I want to touch you."

Rhys swallowed. He hesitated before biting his lower lip and dipping his chin.

Wade took Rhys's mouth with his own once more. It was only a handful of seconds before Rhys fell back under the spell of their kiss. Wade pulled Rhys's zipper down and gently ran the back of his hand across the swollen, covered shaft straining against thin cotton. Rhys groaned and jerked against him.

Blood thundered in Wade's ears as he slipped his hand inside Rhys's briefs and palmed Rhys's naked cock. It was the first time he was touching another man's dick. Specifically, it was the first time he was touching his best friend's dick.

It felt fucking sublime.

Wade's eyes widened as he stroked his palm and fingers up and down Rhys's hot shaft, measuring his length and thickness.

Rhys writhed and bucked against Wade. He pulled back from their kiss and arched his neck, color staining his skin a dull pink. His eyes closed and his lips parted on a throaty whimper as Wade continued working him.

Wade pushed up slightly on his knees and looked down between their bodies.

"Shit," he said hoarsely.

Rhys's engorged cock was a beautiful, flushed color where it glistened with pre-cum in Wade's grip. Wade flicked the pad of his thumb across the milky drops pearling at the head and was rewarded with a guttural cry that came from deep inside Rhys's chest.

Wade could smell Rhys's musky scent. And it was driving him wild. He dropped hot kisses on Rhys's throat as he accelerated the motion of his wrist, rubbing and kneading Rhys's inflamed flesh faster and faster, occasionally lowering his fingers to squeeze the tightening sac beneath. Wade cursed as his gaze returned again and again to the intoxicating sight of his own fingers playing Rhys's hot, twitching length.

"*Wade!*" Rhys moaned. "I'm gonna—*fuck*, I'm gonna—"

Wade looked up into Rhys's tortured expression. Rhys had opened his eyes and was staring straight at Wade, his pupils dilated and glazed with pleasure.

"Come," Wade rasped. He dropped a kiss on Rhys's lips and circled the pad of his thumb across the sensitive head of Rhys's cock.

Rhys went rigid beneath him. He stopped breathing for a second, his jaw clenching while his spine bowed off the couch, his body pushing Wade up slightly.

He came while crying out Wade's name, his cock jerking and pulsing as he convulsed, shivers coursing uncontrollably through his body.

Wade shuddered when Rhys's thick, hot cum filled his hand.

&

Sweat beaded Rhys's upper lip as he panted, his labored breathing matching the wild pounding of his heart. His body felt like treacle and his brain like mush after the blistering orgasm Wade had just delivered with his hand.

Oh.

Rhys blinked slowly and gazed at Wade where he lay atop him. He glanced down at Wade's hand. His very wet hand.

"I'm—"

"Shit. Don't you dare say you're sorry," Wade murmured. He kissed Rhys before sitting up and grabbing a tissue from a dispenser on a side table.

Rhys propped himself up on his elbows and watched Wade wipe the sticky evidence of his orgasm from his hand. His gaze dropped to the large bulge still straining the front of Wade's pants.

"My turn," Rhys said huskily.

Wade's eyes widened when Rhys rose and pushed him against the backrest of the couch before straddling his lap. Wade's hands moved automatically to Rhys's ass. He palmed the firm cheeks and squeezed, eliciting a groan from Rhys.

"I like this position," Wade said with a grin as Rhys started unbuckling his trousers feverishly.

"Oh yeah?" Rhys mumbled. He bit his lower lip when he slipped Wade's zipper down and exposed the thick wedge of Wade's erection behind black briefs.

"Yup," Wade said, his voice dropping an octave. He cursed when Rhys hooked his thumbs into the material and peeled it down his hips.

Rhys's breath caught as Wade's cock sprung free.

Oh God. It's fucking beautiful. And big.

Rhys's hole contracted in anticipation as he studied the length and breadth of Wade's dick. He reached out with trembling fingers and touched the hot, veiny shaft.

Wade hissed and punched his hips up, pushing his cock into Rhys's eager grasp.

One look at Wade's face told Rhys he was far from unnerved by what they were doing. In fact, Rhys couldn't remember ever seeing the intense light burning in Wade's eyes. It took him a couple of seconds to figure out what it was.

Lust. Pure, unadulterated, blazing-hot lust.

And it made him want to do all sorts of wicked things to Wade.

Rhys moved off the couch and dropped down on his knees between Wade's thighs, dying to experience one of his filthiest fantasies.

Wade's eyes widened when Rhys curled his fingers around the base of his thick shaft.

Rhys looked up at Wade, silently seeking his permission.

Wade's breath shuddered out of his lungs. He widened his thighs, reached down with one hand, and rubbed his thumb across Rhys's lower lip, his gaze molten.

It was all the invitation Rhys needed. He leaned forward, opened his mouth, and swallowed Wade's cock whole.

HOLY FUCK!

Wade's balls tightened against his body at the sinful feel of Rhys's mouth engulfing his shaft. He shivered when he felt the sensitive head hit the scorching depths of Rhys's throat.

Rhys curled his clever tongue around Wade's cock, hollowed his cheeks, and dragged his lips along the twitching surface as he pulled his head back, creating the most incredible sucking motion with his jaw.

Wade cursed out loud.

Rhys smiled as he let go of Wade's shaft, the head popping out of his lips with a wet sound.

"Like that?" he murmured.

One of Wade's hands found Rhys's chin while the other gripped his dick and guided it to Rhys's mouth.

"Suck it," Wade growled, pushing the glistening tip between Rhys's lips.

Instead of shocking Rhys, Wade's filthy command made his eyes burn with desire. He grinned, licked the pre-cum oozing out of Wade's cock, and started blowing him like a pro.

As Rhys sucked Wade toward his orgasm, Wade couldn't help thinking that he hadn't seen anything as arousing as Rhys in the throes of passion. And when Wade twisted his fingers in Rhys's hair and guided Rhys's lips to work his dick just the way he liked it, his hips thrusting up powerfully to fuck Rhys's throat, Wade knew no one could ever satisfy him the way Rhys was pleasuring him right now. And when Wade came in Rhys's mouth, his pulsing cock filling Rhys's cheeks with his seed while animal grunts tore out of his throat, the look on Rhys's face made his heart contract with a feeling he'd never experienced before.

CHAPTER NINE

BEST. BLOWJOB. EVER.

Those three words blazed at the forefront of Wade's muddled mind while his heart raced and his chest heaved with his breaths. He shivered when Rhys let go of his spent dick and blinked in time to see Rhys lick his own lips.

The indecent image of Rhys kneeling between Wade's thighs in his custom-made Italian suit, buckle undone and zipper down, his perfect hair mussed by Wade's fingers, made Wade's cock twitch back to life. He leaned down, grabbed the back of Rhys's head, and kissed him hard.

Shit. That's— Wade shuddered when he tasted his cum on Rhys's tongue *—so fucking hot.*

"Let's move this to the bedroom," Wade growled.

Rhys stiffened in his hold. Wade pulled back slowly and stared at him.

"What are we doing?" Rhys said quietly.

Wade's heart sank as he studied Rhys. The passion was fading from Rhys's eyes. In its stead were the emotions Wade had glimpsed before. Painful acceptance. As if what was happening between them was doomed to end before it even started.

"Something we should have done a long time ago," Wade said stiffly, clamping down on the irritation surging through him.

Rhys sighed, adjusted his briefs and zipper, and climbed to his feet. He dragged a hand down his face. "Do you really think you can take me into that bedroom and fuck me, Wade?"

Wade narrowed his eyes. He slipped his dick back in his pants, zipped up, and rose from the couch. "Why are you fighting this?" he bit out.

Rhys's eyes widened. "Why am *I* fighting this? The question is, why aren't *you*? You're the least gay man I know!" He rubbed the back of his neck with one hand and exhaled loudly, frustration darkening his gaze. "You have no idea what happens when two men have sex. I won't get wet like a woman. You'll have to prep me. And it won't feel like fucking a pussy either."

"I know that!" Wade snapped. "I'm not exactly a stranger to anal sex. And I've been doing my research!"

Rhys rocked back on his heels. He gaped at Wade. "Come again?" he spluttered.

"Well, at least one of us would have come again by now had a certain somebody not gone all prissy on me," Wade retorted.

Rhys ignored the taunt. A muscle jumped in his

jawline as he frowned at Wade. "Answer the question, Wade."

Wade ran a hand through his hair and met Rhys's stare head on. "I've been reading up and watching, um, videos."

❧

RHYS BLINKED SLOWLY, DISBELIEF RESONATING THROUGH him at Wade's outrageous admission. "You?"

"Yes."

"Watching gay porn?" Rhys repeated carefully.

"Yeah." Wade's ears reddened slightly.

"And you weren't…disgusted?" Rhys said, arching an eyebrow.

"No," Wade said. He grimaced. "Although some of the stuff was a bit out of my comfort zone."

Rhys hesitated, his heart starting a steady pounding against his ribs. "And the stuff that wasn't?"

Wade's eyes darkened. "It turned me on when I thought of doing them with you."

Rhys's pulse accelerated under Wade's heated gaze. *Fuck. What the hell do I do with that?*

Wade stepped toward Rhys. "I particularly liked all the different…positions."

Rhys's dick throbbed at Wade's husky voice. He could tell Wade was getting aroused again from the way his pupils were dilating.

Wade stopped in front of Rhys. "I didn't know a man's body could be that—," he clutched Rhys's butt in one hand and jerked him forward until their groins met, "—*pliable.*"

Rhys bit back a groan and placed a hand on Wade's chest. "Stop right there. I think we need to lay down some ground rules."

Wade's expression fell so comically Rhys almost laughed out loud.

"What kind of rules?" Wade grumbled. Lines wrinkled his brow in the next instant. "They had better not include stupid shit like no sex before the third date, 'cause I don't think my dick could survive the torture."

Rhys bit his lip to stop himself from grinning. "Well, no, not quite that bad." He sobered as he looked at Wade. "You need to give me some head space. This—," Rhys raised a hand and cupped Wade's cheek gently, "—is happening way too fast for me."

Wade closed his eyes and shuddered. He turned his head and pressed a hot kiss to Rhys's palm before opening his eyes and fixing Rhys with a hard stare.

"Okay," Wade said reluctantly. "But no more running away."

Rhys chewed his lip and dipped his chin.

Wade studied him with a thoughtful frown. "Six weeks."

Rhys blinked. "What?"

"That's my proposition to you," Wade said. "If it makes you more comfortable, we'll try this out until the end of the Osaka project, then…reassess."

Rhys watched him for a silent moment. "Six weeks, huh?" he said finally.

"Yup," Wade said.

Rhys shivered at the light dawning in Wade's eyes.

A wicked smile curved Wade's lips. "And Rhys? You better bring your A game."

***

"Dinner and a movie?" Wade repeated.

"Uh huh," Rhys said.

"Really?"

Rhys sighed at the sarcasm dripping off Wade's words.

It was the day after and they were going over the details of a new contract in Rhys's office.

"I'll make it a chick flick if you're not careful," Rhys warned.

"Alright, alright," Wade muttered. He watched Rhys for a moment. "Is that what you normally do? What you did with—," he grimaced, "—Michael?"

Guilt stabbed through Rhys at the mention of Michael's name. He'd finally called the lawyer last night and had the conversation he'd been putting off since the day before.

"I'm sorry, Michael," Rhys had said quietly. "You don't deserve what happened."

Stilted silence had echoed across the line.

Michael had finally sighed. "I really like you, Rhys. I wanted to take our relationship to the next level. I was going to suggest it that night."

Rhys had closed his eyes and swallowed a curse at Michael's softly spoken confession.

"Is the reason you went out with me because I...look like him?" Michael had asked.

"I—," Rhys had hesitated, "—I can't pretend that wasn't the initial reason why I was attracted to you. But I also genuinely like you as a person."

"How long have you been in love with him?" Michael had asked after a pause.

Rhys had straightened on his bed at the question. "Twelve years," he'd finally admitted in a low voice.

"Shit," Michael said. A bitter chuckle sounded on the line. "I can't compete with that."

Rhys's nails bit into his palm. He'd never felt more of an ass than he did in that moment. "I—"

"It's okay," Michael said in a resigned tone. "The heart wants what the heart wants." He faltered. "Are you two going out?"

"Kinda," Rhys admitted. "We're trying to take things slow."

"But he's straight, right?" Michael said insistently.

Rhys nodded before realizing Michael couldn't see him. "Yes." A wry grimace twisted Rhys's lips. Trust a lawyer to know that instinctively.

"And he wants this? He wants you?" Michael said skeptically.

Rhys had thought of the way Wade had kissed him and touched him in the last two days. "Apparently, yes," he'd admitted, hoping his voice did not reflect his own doubts.

"Be careful, Rhys," Michael had said before they ended their call. "If you ever need to talk, I'm here."

Rhys gazed at Wade presently and finally answered his question. "Sometimes."

Wade raised an eyebrow. "And the other times?"

Rhys shrugged. "We just met up at a hotel and fucked."

Wade scowled. "Shit."

"Now you know how I felt every time you disappeared off with the wettest pussy you could get your hands on," Rhys said tartly.

"Fuck," Wade said.

CHAPTER TEN

Wade studied Rhys as the latter ordered popcorn and drinks from the concession stand. It was Saturday night and they'd just had dinner at one of Wade's favorite restaurants in midtown.

Rhys had turned up for their date in a white dress shirt and casual, gray pants. He'd completed the look with a dark blazer and a blue scarf that highlighted his eyes.

Wade couldn't help notice the flattering looks the other diners in the restaurant had cast at Rhys while they were having dinner.

Well, he is stunning. And clever. And charming. And he has the most perfect ass I've ever seen.

Wade had swallowed a curse when he'd felt his dick throb beneath the table. He'd spent the next hour of their meal convincing his hard cock that it wasn't going to get any action tonight. Which was a pity, considering how hot Rhys was looking.

"Here," Rhys said presently, plonking a popcorn box in Wade's hand. "Salted caramel."

Surprise flashed through Wade.

"You remembered," he murmured as he followed Rhys into the cinema.

"Well, yeah," Rhys said, ears flushing slightly.

Damn. He's fucking adorable.

"You know—," Wade leaned forward and brought his lips to Rhys's right ear as they entered the movie theater, "—that's kind of what you taste like. Salted caramel. I just realized."

He was rewarded by Rhys shivering and casting him a heated look over his shoulder. Wade's eyes widened when Rhys guided him to the rows at the back.

"Here?" Wade glanced at the distant screen. "You sure?"

"Yeah," Rhys said.

The movie was the latest action blockbuster out of Hollywood. Thirty minutes into the film, Wade's attention and that of his dick started wandering to the man sitting next to him once more. Rhys had slouched in his seat and was watching the screen with a focused expression, one arm across his chest and propping an elbow, his chin resting on his folded knuckles.

Or so it seemed anyway.

Rhys glanced at Wade. Wade's breath caught. He was pretty certain he'd read the expression on Rhys's face correctly. Wade's gaze dropped to Rhys's crotch and the unmistakable bulge denting his pants. Wade licked his lips, desire flaring through him.

Yup. He's fucking turned on alright.

Wade almost cursed out loud when Rhys suddenly reached out and ran his left hand up from Wade's right knee to his thigh, kneading his tense muscles. Wade peeked left and right along their row.

They were the only ones in it. The closest people were seated two rows down and to their left.

Is this why he chose—

Wade hissed as Rhys boldly palmed his aching cock through his trousers. He glanced sideways at Rhys and saw the smirk curving his beautiful mouth. Wade rolled his hips up against Rhys's hand and grinned savagely when he saw him bite his lower lip.

The sound of Rhys unbuckling Wade's trousers was lost in the noise of the car chase happening on the screen. Then Rhys was holding Wade's naked cock in his hand and stroking him, his eyes still focused up ahead, the only signs he was aroused the erection tenting his own pants and the slight flare of his nostrils as he breathed heavily. Pleasure slammed through Wade at the sweet friction of Rhys's fingers on his shaft. He swallowed a grunt when Rhys alternated between caressing the sensitive head of his cock and rubbing his twitching length, wrist moving in a skilled motion that made Wade's toes curl.

Wade's breath locked in his throat when Rhys suddenly twisted in his seat and leaned down to take Wade's cock in his mouth. Wade closed his eyes at the sinful move. He laid his arms along the back of the seats on either side of him and held on tight, knowing he was in for one hell of a ride.

Rhys didn't disappoint as he started licking and sucking Wade with his gifted lips and tongue before taking him all the way back into his throat, one hand wrapped tight around the base of Wade's rock-hard shaft.

Wade cursed in a low voice and dropped one hand to Rhys's head. He twisted his fingers in the styled blond locks and felt Rhys groan around his dick as he rolled his hips and started thrusting up. Tension wound through Wade as he fucked Rhys's mouth in the dark movie theater. He'd never been so turned on in his life, and he knew it had as much to do with the man giving him a spectacular blowjob as it did with them performing the illicit act in a public place.

Wade's orgasm soon raced through his clenched balls and belly. He stiffened and grunted as he came in Rhys's mouth, filling Rhys's cheeks with his cum. Rhys gulped and swallowed, his tongue lashing Wade's sensitive dick in exquisite flicks, his breaths washing out through his nose in harsh pants and tickling Wade's groin.

Wade slowly relaxed back down on his seat as the pulses of his orgasm started to fade, his mind numb with pleasure and his body sated for the moment.

Rhys straightened, took a sip from his drink, and flashed a filthy smile at Wade.

This little—

Wade reached out with one hand, unzipped Rhys's slacks, and dipped his fingers inside Rhys's briefs. Rhys shuddered when Wade closed his palm around his engorged dick. He parted his thighs and slouched in his seat as Wade started giving him a hand job, his knuckles whitening where he gripped the arm rests.

It wasn't long before Rhys came. As the first wave of his orgasm sent his hips jerking against Wade's hand, Rhys turned, gripped Wade's shirt, and buried his face against Wade's shoulder. He held on to Wade's chest for dear life as he groaned and panted in pleasure, teeth biting into the material while his hot cum spurted in Wade's cupped palm.

Shit. I'm hard again.

CHAPTER ELEVEN

RHYS HESITATED BEFORE PRESSING THE BUZZER OUTSIDE Wade's apartment. His fingers clenched around the bottle in his hand.

It was the weekend after Wade and he had gone out for a meal and indulged in their illicit sex play at the back of a movie theater.

Wade had invited him over for dinner.

Eating at each other's place was something they used to do when they lived in Chicago and it was a habit they had fallen out of since they'd come to Japan. But tonight was more than just a simple meal between two friends.

It was their second date and Rhys was a mass of nerves.

He'd barely slept the past week, Wade's words after they'd left the movie theater playing over and over again in his mind while he tossed and turned in bed. It was with considerable reluctance that Wade had allowed Rhys to go back to his apartment on his own as they'd stood on the busy midtown street that night.

"I can tell winning you over is going to be hard work," Wade had admitted with a sigh. "I'll let you go tonight, but only if you promise to come over to mine for dinner next Saturday." He'd grimaced briefly. "If I wasn't flying out tomorrow afternoon, I would have you over sooner."

Wade was going to Chicago for the week to take care of some business matters at the branch there.

Rhys had swallowed his misgivings and murmured, "Alright," with a dip of his chin before he'd stepped into the back of a waiting cab.

Wade had leaned down and brushed his lips against Rhys's cheek as he settled on the seat, surprising him.

"Just so we're clear, I'm planning on really enjoying my...*dessert* that night," Wade had murmured tantalizingly in Rhys's ear a second before he straightened and closed the vehicle's door.

Rhys had startled and stared through the window at Wade before the cab pulled away. There was no mistaking the intent in Wade's glittering eyes.

What the promised dessert would entail on the night of their second date had stoked Rhys's imagination to fever pitch for the rest of that week. Despite drowning himself in work and leaving the office late every day, he'd been unable to erase the filthy fantasies that had swamped his mind until the early hours of the morning.

The door to Wade's apartment opened presently before Rhys could fully draw a nervous breath. Wade appeared, a barefoot vision in designer jeans that clung to his long, powerful legs and a white T-shirt that stretched across his broad shoulders and chest, highlighting his toned build.

"Hey," Wade said softly. A sexy smile curved his sculptured lips as he scanned Rhys's pale, striped long-sleeved shirt and navy chinos beneath his winter coat. "Come on in." He stepped aside.

Rhys clamped down on the inane notion that he was about to enter a lion's den and crossed the threshold into Wade's apartment. "Here," he said, handing Wade the bottle while he took his shoes off.

Wade eyed the expensive label with a raised eyebrow. "My favorite red," he murmured, pleased.

"Well, you did say you were making spaghetti and meatballs when I texted earlier," Rhys said, flexing his toes against the heated floor.

"Here, let me get that for you," Wade said as Rhys started to shrug out of his coat. He placed the bottle on the console table in the foyer and came up behind Rhys.

"I can—" Rhys's protest froze on his lips when Wade touched his shoulders.

He shivered as Wade slowly and silently peeled the coat from his body, Wade's long fingers trailing tantalizingly along Rhys's arms while his breaths ruffled the back of Rhys's head. For one wild moment, Rhys thought Wade skimmed his lips lightly across his hair.

Rhys twisted on his heels just as Wade reached past him to hook his coat on a rack, too agitated to stand still. His heart skittered as he found himself toe to toe with Wade, their bodies barely an inch apart. Rhys almost stopped breathing when he locked gaze with Wade. The sexual tension filling the space between them was reflected tenfold in Wade's slate-blue eyes as he stared hotly at Rhys. Rhys inhaled raggedly, half-expecting the air to burn his lungs.

He had never experienced this suffocating pressure before. He felt exposed, raw, as if he were standing naked before Wade while the latter inspected every quivering, bare inch of him. Rhys wondered dizzily if Wade subjected all the women he'd bedded to this intense focus.

"Wine," Rhys finally managed between dry lips, breaking the charged silence. "I'd like some."

Wade blinked, as if coming out of a daze. "Sure," he murmured thickly.

Rhys was conscious of Wade's eyes boring into his back as he turned and padded down the hall to a large, open plan, monochrome kitchen-diner. Wade's apartment overlooked a leafy park in Minato, some five miles from Rhys's own place in the center of the city. Floor-to-ceiling glass walls fronted the luxurious, fifteenth-floor bachelor's pad and offered a dazzling view of Tokyo Tower in the distance above the trees.

Rhys quelled the butterflies in his stomach and headed over to the stove. He lifted the lid off a large stock pot and was rewarded with a billow of steam carrying the fragrant smell of tomato sauce and Italian spices.

"Hmm, gorgeous." Rhys's mouth watered as he

sniffed appreciatively. "I haven't had your meatballs in forever."

Wade chuckled behind him. "You seemed to be enjoying my meatballs just fine last week."

Rhys turned and rolled his eyes at Wade at the juvenile comment. Wade grinned and popped the cork on the bottle of red wine Rhys had brought before setting it to breathe on the white granite island dominating the dark wood floor. He topped up his glass from an open bottle of red and filled a second one for Rhys.

"Here." Wade handed Rhys the glass.

Electric tingles shot up Rhys's arm when their fingers touched briefly. He gripped the glass and took a large sip of the scarlet liquid. Wade's gaze dropped to Rhys's mouth as he swallowed.

"Stop that," Rhys said hoarsely, his skin warming under Wade's potent stare.

Wade cocked an eyebrow. "Stop what?" he taunted.

Rhys bit back a groan. "The way you're looking at me. Like I'm a mouse and you're a big, bad cat."

A sinful smile stretched Wade's lips. "I don't think I've ever been compared to a cat before," he drawled. He stepped up to Rhys and trailed a finger from Rhys's cheek to his chin.

Rhys shivered at the caress, his cock throbbing to life.

"A wolf, yes." Wade leaned in and held Rhys's chin in place while he nuzzled Rhys's right ear with his lips. He bit down gently on the lobe and tugged.

Rhys shuddered and arched his neck to the side,

instinctively offering Wade better access. *Oh fuck. He's going to make me come, right here, right now.*

Wade laughed softly. "A very *hungry* wolf." He pulled back, dropped a kiss on Rhys's forehead, and moved toward the stove. "Let's eat."

Rhys rocked on his heels, startled. He caught the teasing glance Wade cast at him over his shoulder and swallowed a curse.

This asshole is going to be the death of me and my dick.

Rhys found himself relaxing when they sat down at the dining table and dug into the food, their conversation light and flowing as they talked about work. Things had gone well in Chicago, and it looked as if the possibility of opening a branch of their business on the West Coast would soon be a viable option.

"We may have to consider taking on that third partner soon at this rate," Rhys said thoughtfully as he toyed with his wine glass. They'd finished the second bottle of red and he was feeling pretty mellow.

"I think you're right," Wade concurred.

It was something they'd spoken about often since the Asia branch of their business started taking off a few years back. And they both knew the man they wanted for the job. Bringing Gabe Anderson over to the Tokyo branch of Damon & Tucker had always been about more than just a simple promotion. They'd wanted to test the potential candidate they'd had in mind and so far, Gabe had delivered on every aspect of what they wanted in the third person they wished to bring onboard as a partner in their business.

"So, what's for dessert?" Rhys said absentmindedly as he rose from the table and started clearing the dishes. He stiffened slightly when he realized what he had just said. He kept his eyes down as he headed into the kitchen, hoping Wade wouldn't read anything in the innocent question.

"Well, I did discover this little bakery the other day that makes the most amazing salted caramel cheesecake," Wade drawled. He stood and followed Rhys, brushing past him where he'd stopped to place their dirty plates in the sink.

Rhys glanced at Wade as the latter opened the larder fridge and brought out a cake stand. His pulse jumped when Wade set the exquisite looking confection on the island and slowly, deliberately, dipped a finger in the thick cream cheese.

Wade smiled sensually and cocked an eyebrow at Rhys. "Wanna taste?"

Rhys suddenly found it hard to breathe as an electrifying undercurrent filled the air once more. He flushed at the torrid look in Wade's eyes and twisted on his heels to clasp the countertop behind him in a white-knuckled grip when Wade slowly walked over to him, finger aloft.

"Dessert is served," Wade said in a husky voice that shot straight through Rhys's body and made it react in all sorts of wicked ways.

CHAPTER TWELVE

Wade's cock throbbed as he lifted his finger to Rhys's lips. Rhys's eyes flared, his pupils dilating with arousal.

Rhys kept his gaze locked on Wade as his tongue darted out and licked the cream cheese from Wade's skin, his pink flesh deliciously hot and wet. Wade growled at the sexy, filthy sight and pushed his finger inside Rhys's mouth to the second knuckle. Rhys's cheeks hollowed as he closed his eyes and sucked, color painting his cheekbones a dull red while his tongue and lips wrapped skillfully around Wade's forefinger. A low moan vibrated up Rhys's throat and tickled Wade's skin.

Fuck!

Wade wedged his right leg between Rhys's thighs, yanked his finger out of Rhys's mouth, and grabbed Rhys's head with both hands before taking Rhys's lips in a scorching kiss. A hungry groan rumbled out of

Wade's chest as he delved into the hot depths of Rhys's mouth.

It felt like forever since he'd touched and savored Rhys. He tasted wine and salted caramel and Rhys's very own intoxicating essence.

Wade bit down on Rhys's tongue and flexed his thigh, rubbing up against Rhys's rigid erection. The way Rhys shuddered in his arms and grasped his shoulders was Wade's final undoing.

He dropped his hands to Rhys's waist and backed him out of the kitchen, through the lounge, and into the hall leading to his bedroom, all the while maintaining his sensual assault on Rhys's mouth.

Wade had wanted to take things slow tonight. To give Rhys time to adjust to their changing relationship. Wade could sense Rhys still had his guard up and he knew it would take all the patience he possessed to break through the barriers Rhys instinctively put up when Wade got too close.

But patience was the last thing on Wade's mind right now. He could barely breathe, let alone think coherently. Not when he was this close to Rhys and touching and tasting him.

It wasn't until the back of Rhys's knees struck the edge of the super king-size bed dominating the stark masculine space that he finally blinked his glazed eyes open. He stiffened when he registered their destination. He lowered his hands to Wade's chest and pulled back from their kiss.

"Wade, I—" Rhys stammered.

"No more running, Rhys," Wade murmured, fingers

flexing in Rhys's hair as he resisted Rhys's attempt to push him away. He fixed Rhys with a hard stare and nibbled at Rhys's lower lip. "We're doing this."

Rhys's eyes widened when he spotted the bottle of lube and the box of condoms on the nightstand. A gasp left his lips when Wade pressed on his shoulders and forced him gently down on the edge of the bed.

Wade knelt on the mattress on either side of Rhys and crowded him until he lay flat on his back with Wade hunkered down over him.

"Tell me you don't want this and I'll stop," Wade said, eyes boring into Rhys's wild-eyed gaze.

Rhys shivered when Wade ran a finger from the base of his throat and down his body all the way to the bulge straining against his chinos. Rhys licked his lips, clearly struggling to find the words to express the unease reflected in his blue eyes.

Wade knew what Rhys was afraid of. Rhys was running scared because he thought Wade would refuse him. That Wade would be turned off when faced with the reality of actually having sex with him.

Wade clenched his jaw and inhaled shallowly.

If he only knew how turned on I am right now and how much I'm holding back. How badly I want to sink my cock deep inside his body and watch him go wild as I fuck him.

Wade had never felt this way about any of his previous conquests. Never felt this desire to stamp his touch all over another person's body. To possess someone in every sinful meaning of the word.

"I—" Rhys mumbled.

"Yes?" Wade dipped his head and nipped at the edge

of Rhys's left collarbone where it stood exposed at the opening of his shirt.

"Shit," Rhys moaned.

Wade sensed the moment Rhys surrendered from the way his gaze turned to cobalt and his hands rose to clutch at Wade's shoulders once more. Wade fused their mouths together, lowered himself onto Rhys, and was rewarded by a sultry groan that made his dick swell. Wade's voice rumbled out of his throat in an animal sound at the heady feel of Rhys's body under his.

HE'S DRIVING ME INSANE!

Rhys shuddered at the potent weight of Wade's frame crushing him into the bed. He was drowning in Wade's heat and scent, his senses overwhelmed and his will bending like willow to that of the formidable man claiming his lips as if he was the best thing he'd ever tasted. Rhys was conscious of Wade's heavy erection digging insistently in his thigh. Rhys found himself fervently praying Wade's cock would stay that way when Wade finally saw him naked.

Because there was no denying what was about to happen between them. And now that he'd accepted the inescapable truth, Rhys found himself more aroused than he'd ever been in his entire life.

"Let's get this off you," Wade said gruffly against Rhys's lips. He rose onto his knees and straddled Rhys's waist, his fingers moving jerkily to the buttons of Rhys's shirt.

Rhys stroked his hands up Wade's powerful thighs and bit his lip as he eyed the large bulge of Wade's erection. He undid the top button of Wade's jeans and slid the zipper down, the sound loud and thrilling above the blood pounding in his ears.

Fire scorched Rhys's skin when Wade yanked his shirt open and leaned down to drop a kiss on his chest. Wade's lips moved to Rhys's left nipple. He flicked his tongue across the hardened nub and kissed it before tugging on it with his teeth.

"*Fuck!*" Rhys cursed. He arched helplessly beneath Wade, his eyes glazing over at the sharp pleasure-pain of the sting.

Wade straightened and took Rhys's shirt off hastily before ridding him of the rest of his clothes, his hands rough as he peeled Rhys's chinos and briefs off Rhys's legs. Wade stepped off the bed, yanked his T-shirt over his head, and stripped out of his jeans and briefs.

Rhys froze as he took in Wade's naked body for the first time in the soft glow of the bedside lamps. He'd seen Wade in swim trunks before but had never appreciated how powerful an impact the man he'd lusted after all these years would have in the nude. Wade was all hard planes and angles, his broad shoulders and chest tapering down to his defined abs and the deep V leading to his groin. Dark curls dusted his pecs and nipples before arrowing down to a sexy strip that framed his belly button and merged sinfully with his trimmed pubes.

Rhys's pulse stuttered when he eyed Wade's impressive erection and heavy balls. *Thank God he's still hard!*

Rhys's hole contracted tightly at the thought of taking Wade's cock. He knew instinctively it would be the best and most filling fuck he would ever have.

Wade's voice jolted Rhys out of his filthy daydream.

"Like what you see?" Wade said thickly.

Wade's gaze skimmed Rhys from the top of his head all the way to his toes as he dented the mattress with his knees and climbed on the bed again. His eyes had turned a stormy blue, the gunmetal specks in his irises glittering so hotly Rhys found it a miracle he hadn't melted beneath them.

How Rhys kept himself from squirming under Wade's heated stare he didn't know. Then he stopped thinking, stopped breathing as Wade crawled up on top of him.

"I gotta say, I'm loving what I'm seeing," Wade murmured. "You're fucking gorgeous, Rhys."

Rhys bit his lower lip. He'd been called many things by his previous lovers. Gorgeous wasn't one of them.

"I especially like the color of your dick," Wade continued in a low voice. He reached down and trailed his left forefinger along Rhys's hard length, making him curse again. "All rosy and flushed. It makes me want to know what it'll taste like."

CHAPTER THIRTEEN

WADE'S HEART POUNDED AGAINST HIS RIBS AS HE watched Rhys's lips part on a shocked inhale. He caressed Rhys's twitching length again and bit back a curse when Rhys shuddered and tensed at his touch.

So beautiful.

Wade had been deadly serious when he'd told Rhys he was gorgeous. Although he was used to a woman's shape and curves, Wade was fascinated by the rugged lines of Rhys's body. Rhys's frame was shorter and narrower than Wade's. Wade knew Rhys kept himself fit by running and swimming and he could tell from Rhys's toned muscles and softly defined six-pack that Rhys took pride in keeping his body in shape.

Wade couldn't wait to find out how Rhys would feel in his embrace. And he had every intention of tasting him everywhere. With that blistering thought in mind, Wade closed his palm around Rhys's cock and took Rhys's mouth in a demanding kiss as he started working Rhys's quivering shaft, his grip slick with Rhys's pre-cum.

Rhys gasped against Wade's lips and gripped the bedsheets, his eyes fluttering closed while his tongue clashed against Wade's, responding to the fierce mating dance.

Wade took one of Rhys's hands and brought it to his shoulder. "Touch me," he ordered roughly.

Rhys blinked, fingers flexing in Wade's skin. He shivered and gripped Wade's shoulders with both hands as the latter continued stroking him.

Wade wrenched his mouth from Rhys's and nudged Rhys's chin up, seeking access to Rhys's throat. Rhys twisted his head to the side, his lips opening on a low moan as Wade rained blistering kisses down his neck.

Wade paused over Rhys's fluttering pulse and sucked gently on his skin before sinking his teeth into Rhys's flesh, his own cock twitching between his thighs as Rhys's unique essence hit his taste buds and the musky scent of his arousal swamped his senses.

Rhys cried out and jerked beneath him at the love bite, his nails biting into Wade's shoulders.

Shit. Wade shuddered. *I want him to do that when I'm inside him one day. Score my back with his nails while I drive him out of his mind.*

Wade struggled to calm his raging libido and throbbing dick as he started working his way down Rhys's body, exploring his hot, trembling, golden skin, the smattering of blond hair covering Rhys's firm chest tickling his lips. He kept one hand on Rhys's dick as he explored Rhys's nipples and quickly discovered how much he seemed to enjoy having his hard, sensitive nubs played with. When Wade opened his mouth wide and sucked on Rhys's left pec, a guttural sound left Rhys and his cock pulsated wildly between Wade's fingers.

Wade growled and repeated the movement with Rhys's right pec.

Rhys stiffened beneath Wade.

Wade blinked and looked down at Rhys's trembling, hard shaft while Rhys panted beneath him. Sweat beaded Rhys's face and his entire body twitched and quivered, his baby blue eyes sultry with pleasure as he blinked them open.

"Did you just have a dry orgasm?" Wade asked huskily.

RHYS LOOKED DAZEDLY AT WADE, HIS PULSE RACING IN his veins. He couldn't believe he had come so fast from Wade's touch and kiss.

"I—hmm, yes," Rhys breathed, still stunned by his body's reaction. He could count on the fingers of one hand how many partners he'd had who had been able to draw out a dry orgasm from him. And none of them had done it as quickly as the man currently staring passionately at him.

Wade's eyes darkened. "Shit. That's so—"

Rhys moaned as Wade let go of his sensitive cock and continued working his way feverishly down his body, his fingers, lips, and tongue scorching a fiery trail along Rhys's heated skin that made Rhys gasp and writhe on the bed.

Rhys's eyes widened when Wade kissed and sucked the trembling flesh of his lower abdomen. He lifted his head off the mattress a second before Wade's hot breath washed across his engorged dick.

"Wade, you don't have to—," Rhys mumbled. "*Oh fuck!*" He dropped back down on the bed and fisted his hands in the sheets at the shocking feel of Wade's mouth on his hard shaft.

Pleasure slammed through Rhys as Wade licked and sucked him from the sensitive head of his cock down to his tight balls.

I'm dreaming right now! There is no way this is really happening. That he's—

"*Wade!*" Rhys cried out, his hands leaving the bedsheets to grasp the head of the man crouched between his thighs and going down on him in a spectacularly filthy fashion. Wade's lips and tongue wrapped around Rhys's length and he swallowed him inside the scalding, velvety depths of his mouth.

Rhys's eyes nearly rolled into the back of his head when Wade started sucking him in earnest. He shuddered and arched, shivers wracking his tense frame, his teeth biting so hard into his lower lip he almost drew blood.

When Wade stroked and fondled Rhys's balls before taking his dick all the way to the back of his throat, Rhys lost it. He fisted his fingers in Wade's thick hair, dug his heels into the mattress on either side of Wade's knees, and started thrusting up. Incoherent cries left

Rhys's lips as he gave in to his body's primal urges and fucked Wade's mouth and throat.

Wade gripped Rhys's dancing hips, his head bobbing up and down on Rhys's throbbing cock, working him harder and faster.

The first wave of Rhys's orgasm danced down his spine and pulsed through his twitching hole.

"I'm gonna—*Wade*, I'm gonna—," Rhys moaned and panted. He pulled at Wade's head, trying to get him off.

An animal groan left Wade. He resisted Rhys's attempt to pull him off, his fingers biting punishingly into Rhys's flesh. He tugged on Rhys's cock with his lips and grazed his teeth along the sensitive shaft.

Rhys's spine bowed off the bed as he climaxed violently. His breath froze in his lungs for a timeless moment before it left his body in a long, low guttural sound. Fierce shudders coursed through him as his cock pulsed and jerked inside Wade's mouth.

A ringing noise filled Rhys's ears when he finally collapsed down on the bed, his body drenched in sweat and his mind fuzzy with pleasure. Rhys moaned when Wade finally let go of his spent cock. He blinked his eyes open and gazed groggily at the man climbing up over him.

CHAPTER FOURTEEN

WADE LICKED HIS LIPS, THE POTENT TASTE OF RHYS'S cum still on his tongue. He decided there and then that blowing Rhys was fast going to become one of his favorite activities. He'd gone down on plenty of women before but giving head to a man, *this* man, took the experience to another level.

The feel of Rhys's rock hard, thick shaft filling Wade's mouth while he licked and sucked it. The heat and silky smoothness of his quivering organ as his pre-cum coated Wade's tongue. The way Rhys had surrendered to his most primitive compulsion and plunged his dick repeatedly all the way to the back of Wade's throat. Wade wanted to experience all of it again and soon.

He shuddered as he looked into Rhys's pleasure-dazed eyes. *But before that, I need to do something about my own dick before it blows. And the only place I want to come tonight is inside his tight ass.*

"That was—," Rhys murmured. He paused and swallowed convulsively.

"Sexy as fuck," Wade growled. He grabbed Rhys's waist and rolled him onto his front.

Rhys gasped when Wade moved over him and plastered his body to Rhys's, his chest kissing Rhys's sweat slicked back, his dick cradled by the plump curves of Rhys's butt, his heavy frame pushing Rhys into the mattress.

Wade took Rhys's hands in his own and slid them up above Rhys's head. He nuzzled Rhys's nape and savored the heady sensation of having Rhys under him for a moment before he rolled his hips.

Rhys moaned as Wade rubbed his entire body up and down the back of his. His fingers squeezed the sheets under Wade's grip and he bowed his head into the bed, exposing the delicious arch of his nape.

"Shit, Rhys," Wade groaned, "I want inside you so bad." He bit the flesh of Rhys's neck and was rewarded with a breathless curse as Rhys panted and shuddered, his flushed skin scorching hot against Wade's lips. Wade pushed up slightly on his elbows and positioned his aching cock in the groove of Rhys's butt cheeks. He started flexing his hips in a rousing bump and grind that had his pre-cum leaking all over Rhys's enticing crack and Rhys twitching and whimpering beneath him.

Wade could feel his self-control slipping as he moved down Rhys's body.

More. I want more!

Rhys tensed when Wade palmed his butt cheeks and

slid his thumbs in the groove separating them. "Wade," he breathed, his knuckles whitening in the bedsheets.

Wade wasn't sure if Rhys was warning him or begging him. In that moment, Wade didn't care. Nothing was going to stop him from uncovering Rhys's most intimate part. The place he was dying to bury his cock so deep into he might decide to stay there forever.

Wade sank his teeth in Rhys's right butt cheek and bit him gently, deliberately prolonging the torturous foreplay. Rhys cursed and arched up into him. Wade kissed and laved the tender love bite with his tongue before doing the same to Rhys's left butt. Rhys moaned and punched his hips jerkily into the bed.

Wade finally gave in to his desire and slowly spread Rhys's ass. His breath caught when he exposed Rhys's hole.

Fuck.

Wade's heated gaze roamed the quivering, pink pucker. Before he knew it, Wade found himself leaning down and flicking his tongue against the tight folds.

He might as well have set off a bomb the way Rhys reacted to that move. A hoarse cry left Rhys's lips as he went rigid beneath Wade. He convulsed in the next moment, the shivers wracking his body telling Wade that he had just had another dry orgasm. Wade grunted and started kissing and licking Rhys's hole in earnest while the waves of the latter's climax still coursed through him, impatiently preparing his entrance for what was to follow.

Rhys whimpered and trembled beneath him, his body limp with pleasure.

Wade rose on his knees, grabbed the lube and a condom, and rapidly sheathed his aching cock. He yanked a pillow close and positioned it under Rhys's belly, raising Rhys's butt up in the air. Blood thundered in Wade's ears as his frantic gaze roamed the exquisite line of Rhys's back where the latter lay submissively on the bed.

Rhys turned his head and looked at Wade over his shoulder. His burning cobalt stare and the way he bit his lower lip as his gaze dropped to Wade's sheathed cock drew a lustful groan from Wade.

If I don't get inside him in the next five minutes, I'm going to explode!

He poured a liberal amount of lube onto his shaft and in his right hand before parting Rhys's butt cheeks with his left hand and bringing his wet fingers to Rhys's hole.

Rhys moaned as Wade started stroking and circling his twitching folds. Air left his throat in a delicious hiss seconds later when Wade probed his entrance with his right thumb. His hole spasmed and unfurled.

Wade cursed as he stared at where his thumb was disappearing inside Rhys's tight passage. He started finger-fucking Rhys's opening, dipping his slick thumb in and out and twisting it around, stretching the tight rings of muscles he could feel squeezing him. His dick pulsed and leaked pre-cum inside the condom at the thought of penetrating Rhys's most sinful part.

Wade slipped his thumb out of Rhys's spasming

channel and pushed his right forefinger and middle finger in. Rhys grunted and arched up against Wade's hand, his body swallowing Wade's fingers all the way to the knuckles, his hips rolling and rubbing his cock on the pillow. A hoarse shout ripped out of Rhys when the tips of Wade's fingers rolled across the soft bump of his prostate. Wade groaned and scissored his fingers inside Rhys, spreading him wide while repeatedly stroking his pleasure spot.

Wade's pounding heart sent red pulses across his vision as he yanked his fingers out of Rhys, knelt over him, and guided his rock-hard dick to Rhys's hole, his fingers trembling and his breaths coming in heavy pants.

He had never wanted to fuck anyone as badly as he wanted to fuck Rhys at that moment.

Rhys stiffened when Wade probed his opening with the broad head of his cock. Wade grabbed Rhys's hands where he'd twisted them in the sheets and crowded Rhys's back with his chest, his knees on either side of Rhys's thighs.

They both groaned as Wade slowly pushed his throbbing shaft into Rhys's body, his hips moving in steady thrusts.

Wade stilled when he was all the way in to the hilt. He closed his eyes and inhaled shakily, sweat dripping off his face as he soaked in the incredible sensation of being inside Rhys. Rhys's passage was tight and snug around his swollen dick, the rings of muscles protecting his entrance a taut band that compressed and sucked at Wade's flesh. Wade could tell from the way Rhys lay motionless beneath him, his thundering heart echoing through his back and thumping against Wade's chest while his breaths came in shallow pants, that he was similarly overwhelmed by this incredible moment.

Wade knew then that no one would ever be as precious to him as the man currently lying against him, body and soul bared vulnerably to Wade as they engaged in this most primal of acts.

Wade buried his face in Rhys's neck, pulled his cock out of Rhys's hole, and drove it back into Rhys all the way to the hilt.

"Fuck!" Rhys moaned, his channel spasming deliciously around Wade's shaft.

Wade growled as he set a hard, punishing pace from the get go, his hips flexing and rolling deeply as he gave Rhys what they both so badly wanted. Rhys squirmed and arched beneath him, his ass rising to meet Wade's increasingly wild thrusts, his mouth open on breathless gasps and moans.

Pleasure pulsed savagely through Wade, robbing him of breath. Of thought.

Nothing existed outside this mad, primitive moment of give and take, of thrust and penetration, of possession and surrender.

I want to see! I want to see him when I come inside him!

Wade clenched his jaw as he pulled out of Rhys. He flipped Rhys onto his back, grabbed Rhys's calves, and yanked him close. He hooked Rhys's legs around his waist and froze when he got his first look at Rhys.

Shit!

Passion darkened Rhys's eyes and painted red flags across his cheekbones. He gazed at Wade with a hungry, sultry expression, his lower lip red and swollen where he'd bitten into it.

"Wade," Rhys breathed, his voice full of need as he rolled his hips against Wade's groin.

Wade cursed as Rhys rubbed his wet hole against Wade's heavy balls and the back of his engorged dick. Wade guided his cock to Rhys's opening and slid all the way inside in a single, hard thrust that wrenched the loudest cry yet from Rhys's lips.

Wade leaned up over Rhys and took his mouth in a blistering kiss as he started their primal mating dance once more, his cock plunging powerfully in and out of Rhys's body while the latter's dick jerked and leaked pre-cum all over Wade's abdomen.

Wade pinned Rhys's hands above his head and fucked him harder and deeper than he'd ever fucked anyone.

Rhys came just as Wade's own climax started spiraling through his spine and balls and pooled deep inside his lower belly. Wade swallowed Rhys's cries of pleasure as the latter shuddered and shook beneath him, his hole contracting exquisitely on Wade's dick and drawing a guttural groan from deep inside Wade's chest, his heels digging sweetly into Wade's lower back, his hot cum mixing with the sweat drenching their bodies.

Wade stiffened as the first wave of his orgasm shivered across his skin. He gripped Rhys's fingers tightly in his own, his hips accelerating in an uncontrollable frenzy while the most mind-blowing pleasure swelled inside him. The bed rocked as he lost control, animal grunts leaving his throat and matching his rough, uneven movements. He rose above Rhys, his spine arching as his climax rolled over him, his feverish gaze finding the face of the man who was bringing him to such ecstasy.

Rhys's pleasure glazed expression and glittering blue eyes was everything Wade could have wished for in that timeless moment of perfection.

CHAPTER FIFTEEN

 racing pulse impossibly fast as he looked up dazedly at Wade while the latter finally stilled above him, sweat-slicked face flushed and slate-blue eyes dark and sensual from his powerful climax.

Though Rhys had dreamt about having sex with Wade for over a decade, none of his fantasies even came close to matching the earth-shattering reality of the act. Never in his entire adult life had Rhys experienced such mind-numbing orgasms as the ones he'd just had in Wade's arms. He was amazed he was still conscious considering how high Wade had taken him during their wild ride.

Rhys moaned when Wade carefully pulled out of him and discarded the used condom. Pulses of pleasure darted through his sensitive passage, his sphincter contracting and already missing the thick intruder that had just so thoroughly fucked him. Wade lowered his frame onto Rhys and pressed him into the mattress before taking his lips with his own.

Emotion clogged Rhys's throat, his heart melting at the slow, tender kiss.

Wade buried his face in the crook of Rhys's neck and let out a ragged sigh, his heartbeat drumming rapidly against Rhys's chest.

"As soon as I can get my dick up, we're doing that again," Wade murmured thickly.

Rhys shivered when Wade's hot breath tickled his skin. "Oh yeah?"

"Most definitely," Wade growled, nibbling on Rhys's flesh. "I am never going to get enough of *that*. Ever."

Rhys chuckled, the undercurrent of anxiety that had plagued him all day easing at Wade's fervent words. His worse fears hadn't come true. Wade had not only maintained his erection but he'd given Rhys the best fuck he had ever received. And he seemed to have enjoyed it just as much as Rhys had.

Wade pushed up on his elbows a moment later and dropped a kiss on the tip of Rhys's nose. "Ready for round two?" he said with a wicked smile.

Rhys blinked when he felt Wade's thick, hard, and most definitely erect cock pushing insistently against his belly. He groaned. "What are you, a beast?"

Wade chuckled and rained hot kisses down Rhys's throat and chest. "Looks like we're going to have to work on someone's stamina," he murmured teasingly.

Rhys frowned. "There's nothing wrong with my stamina. It's yours that I'm—," he gasped when Wade tugged on his left nipple with his teeth before reaching down to rub the back of his knuckles along Rhys's twitching cock, "—*fuck*, worried about!"

Wade suddenly pulled back and climbed off the bed.

Rhys blinked rapidly, stunned by the sudden feeling of loss that swept over him as Wade's warmth faded from his skin. "Wade?" he mumbled, a sliver of fear flaring through him as he watched Wade head for the door stark naked.

Wade stopped and grinned at him over his shoulder. "I've just had an idea." He exited the bedroom, soft footsteps fading as he padded down the hall.

Rhys tried to calm his racing heart as he lay back down on Wade's bed, puzzled by what Wade meant. He didn't have to wait long to find out.

Rhys's eyes widened when Wade returned seconds later with the cheesecake stand in hand. "Oh."

Wade placed the cake on the nightstand, dipped his finger in the thick cream cheese, and climbed back on the bed. He straddled Rhys's body and gave him the most sexy, sinful grin Rhys had ever seen on another human being before deliberately smearing the white cream on Rhys's nipples.

Rhys gasped at the cool sensation. His breath locked in his throat in the next instant as Wade swiped more cream off the cake and coated Rhys's quivering cock with it.

"We couldn't exactly let it go to waste now, could we?" Wade said huskily before dipping his head and lashing at Rhys's nipples with his tongue. He licked the cream clean and moved down to Rhys's cock.

Sweet Mother of God!

❧

SOFT LIGHT FLUTTERED ACROSS WADE'S EYELIDS. HE sighed, rolled onto his side, and slowly blinked his eyes open. His breath caught and his heart stuttered at the sight before him.

Rhys lay asleep on his front next to him, his normally immaculate blond hair mussed up in the most adorable way, his lips parted slightly on slow, steady breaths.

Wade relaxed down into the bed. It was the first time in years that he'd woken up with someone at his side. That that someone was Rhys didn't feel odd. If anything, it felt strangely fitting. As if this was the way it was always meant to be.

Funny thing is, that should scare the shit out of me. But it doesn't.

Wade allowed this startling realization to sink in before he slowly propped himself up on his right elbow. He followed the delicious curve of Rhys's back with his eyes before it disappeared under the sheet hugging his waist. Wade stared at Rhys to make sure he was still fast asleep before carefully hooking his left index finger in the sheet and drawing it back. He swallowed a groan as he exposed the hard lines of Rhys's hips and thighs and the tantalizing mounds of his ass.

They'd had sex another half a dozen times last night after Wade lathered Rhys's body with cream cheese and took his sweet time driving Rhys utterly wild with his lips and tongue before drawing Rhys onto his hands and knees and fucking him doggy style. Rhys had gone down on Wade in the shower and given him another spectacular blow job. Wade had reciprocated by lifting Rhys up against the black slate wall and fucking him under the pounding water, Rhys's cries echoing loudly around them while he scored Wade's back with his nails. They'd changed the bedsheets before falling back into each other's arms, their passion unabated as they took their time exploring each other's bodies. It didn't take long for their lust to get the better of them and they mated with a fierceness that bordered on the savage as night gradually gave way to dawn.

Wade could see the mark he'd made with his teeth on Rhys's right butt cheek. He was suddenly filled with the urge to kiss it. He cast a final glance at Rhys and was inches away from fusing his greedy lips to Rhys's golden curves when a sleepy voice made him freeze.

"What the hell are you doing?" Rhys mumbled.

CHAPTER SIXTEEN

Wade looked around and met Rhys's puzzled stare. He flashed him a brazen smile. "Busted."

Rhys sighed and rolled onto his back, the sheet tangling sexily around his waist and thighs. "You were about to bite my ass again, weren't you? Is there something you need to confess, Wade? Like an ass fetish or something?"

Wade crawled up the bed and propped himself on his elbows next to Rhys. "I take offense at that. The only ass I'm obsessed with is yours. And I was about to kiss it better." He lowered his head and took Rhys's mouth in a slow, soft kiss that had Rhys's eyes fluttering closed and his hands rising to grip Wade's head. "Good morning," Wade murmured throatily.

Rhys blinked his eyes open slowly, his expression dazed. "Good morning," he breathed. "I swear you're a goddamn magician," he added with a groan.

"Why? Have I bewitched you?" Wade asked, his light tone masking the sudden seriousness of his question.

Rhys studied him for a moment. "Yes. Utterly," he said quietly before pulling the sheet back and climbing off the bed.

Wade's heart twisted at the bittersweet expression he glimpsed in Rhys's eyes. He rolled onto his back and watched Rhys walk over to the windows and pull the curtains fully open, exposing a glorious, sunny winter morning.

Wade folded his hands behind his head and settled on the pillow, his gaze roaming the back of Rhys's body admiringly as the latter stood and stretched his arms above his shoulders, his naked silhouette highlighted by the golden light flooding the bedroom.

Rhys looked over his shoulder and raised an eyebrow at Wade. "So, what have you got planned for the day?"

You. I want to do you. Over and over again until your voice is hoarse and I can't get my dick up.

Wade sensed this was not quite the answer Rhys was looking for. He sighed, told his raging erection it was unlikely to see any action this morning, and smiled faintly at Rhys.

"Fancy pancakes?" he drawled.

Rhys narrowed his eyes. "You mean, your homemade ones? You know I'd kill for those." A grimace twisted his lips. "Although I'm not sure I have space for anything sweet after last night's, er, cake fest." He patted his trim belly.

"To be fair, I did have most of it," Wade said, his cock doing push-ups between his thighs at the memory of the addictive combination of salted caramel cheesecake and Rhys. "And we can always, you know —," he waggled his eyebrows suggestively at Rhys, "— burn off some of the calories after."

Rhys chuckled, the sound so light and carefree it made Wade's chest grow warm with affection. "You're incorrigible, you know that?"

Wade grinned. "You mean, as in I see what I want and I go after it?"

Rhys shook his head lightly. "Something like that." His gaze dropped. "I think I should take care of you first, though, don't you?"

Wade's pulse picked up speed as Rhys strolled back to the bottom of the bed, baby blue eyes sparkling with amusement while he inspected the tent Wade's erect cock had made of the sheet covering his lower body. Rhys flashed Wade a filthy grin before lifting the cotton and crawling under it.

Shit.

Wade shuddered when Rhys settled between his thighs under the sheet and wrapped his hot lips and tongue around Wade's aching cock. Wade made himself comfortable on the bed and watched the shape of Rhys's head bob up and down as he started blowing Wade. He closed his eyes and gave in to the pleasure Rhys was giving him, only to blink when Rhys released his stiff cock a moment later. Wade stared, puzzled, as Rhys yanked the sheet off the both of them and straddled his waist.

Rhys grabbed the lube from the nightstand, his expression feverish and his lips slick with Wade's pre-cum. He opened the bottle and poured a liberal amount of the liquid in his left hand.

Wade's eyes widened when Rhys palmed his saliva-slicked cock and coated it liberally with the lube. His breath locked in his lungs in the next instant as Rhys squatted above him and offered him a rousing view of his dick and balls and the tantalizing area beneath. Rhys breathed heavily as he placed his right hand on Wade's chest for support and brought his lubed fingers to his hole, his cheeks flushed and his eyes bright with the same lust burning through Wade.

Wade gaped, mesmerized, as Rhys started rubbing and playing with himself. A lightheaded feeling washed over him when Rhys pushed his index finger inside himself and started thrusting.

Holy fuck!

Wade sat up and reached for Rhys, impatient to touch him. Rhys shook his head and pushed him down onto the bed with his hand.

"No!" Rhys grunted. "Just—watch!"

Blood pounded in Wade's ears as Rhys slipped a second, then a third digit inside himself, his lips parted on delicious moans while his hips rolled in perfect synchrony to the sinful finger fuck he was giving himself.

Rhys suddenly gasped and straightened before moving his right hand from Wade's chest to the mattress between Wade's thighs, his head falling back as he leaned away from Wade.

Wade shuddered at the incredible view before him. He could see every single detail of Rhys's trembling body as Rhys continued to pleasure himself, hips punching and knees flexing as he bobbed above Wade, his butt nudging and bumping Wade's erection.

From Rhys's hard nipples and the thin film of sweat coating his arched throat and chest. From the quivering, toned muscles of his lower abdomen to his jerking cock and twitching balls. From his lube-slick fingers to the delicious pink folds of his spasming hole.

"Rhys," Wade hissed between gritted teeth, his knuckles whitening on the sheet.

He was seconds away from pushing Rhys down on the bed and shoving his throbbing cock inside him.

Rhys straightened his head and looked down at Wade with a glazed expression. He slipped his fingers out, grabbed Wade's dick, and aligned it with his hole.

Is he really gonna—

Wade's pulse skittered when he met Rhys's gaze. He could see the wicked answer to his unspoken question in the molten, cobalt depths staring at him.

Rhys bit his lip and slowly pushed down onto the head of Wade's cock.

Wade cursed and grabbed Rhys's waist, his avid eyes taking in the incredible sight of his naked dick disappearing inside Rhys's tight, hot passage.

He couldn't believe Rhys was taking him bareback. The last time Wade had fucked anyone without a condom was when he was still a stupid, horny teenager.

Rhys pressed both hands on Wade's chest and rose up on his heels, lifting himself off Wade's thick shaft until only the head of Wade's dick stretched his entrance. He stared hotly at Wade and sank slowly back down, impaling himself on Wade's cock.

Wade grunted at the exquisite sight and feel of Rhys's opening swallowing his cock whole again, the taut rim dragging torturously on the sensitive, veiny skin of his shaft. He cursed when Rhys repeated the move.

"Wade!" Rhys panted. He bowed his head and bobbed rhythmically up and down on Wade's cock, his fingers digging into Wade's chest where he clung to him.

Pleasure slammed through Wade as Rhys danced and undulated above him. He flexed his fingers bitingly into Rhys's flesh and started thrusting up, his powerful movements matching Rhys's downward motions. Rhys cried out as Wade's cock repeatedly rubbed against his prostate.

By the time Wade's mind-numbing climax spiraled through his belly and balls, he'd brought Rhys to two dry orgasms. Wade gnashed his teeth and fixed Rhys's hips in place while he shoved his aching cock harder and faster into Rhys's hole, his heated stare locked on Rhys's pleasure-glazed eyes.

Rhys's face twisted in a mask of ecstasy when he finally came, his dick splashing cum all the way up Wade's chest to his neck, his shouts echoing in Wade's ears, his passage contracting deliciously around Wade's shaft with the violent pulses of his explosive orgasm.

Wade groaned, his own climax surging through him. He bowed his spine and grunted as he came inside Rhys.

Rhys whimpered and trembled violently above him, clearly overwhelmed by the sensation of Wade filling him with his cum.

An animal sound ripped out of Wade's chest when he saw the evidence of his orgasm coat Rhys's opening in a pale, sticky ring. The obscene, wet sounds of friction his and Rhys's bodies made as he continued plunging his dick in and out of Rhys's passage unravelled the last of Wade's control. He sat up, grabbed Rhys's head in his hands, and yanked Rhys's face down before crushing their mouths together, desperate to taste him in the same way his cock was tasting Rhys's most intimate part.

Rhys gasped and moaned, his hands rising to clutch Wade's shoulders while his hips slowly shuddered and jerked to a stop. Wade lashed his tongue gently against Rhys's while the latter collapsed languidly in his arms, Wade's cock still buried deep inside him.

Wade finally let go of Rhys's mouth and pressed their foreheads together, their ragged breaths warming each other's skin.

"That was fucking unreal," Wade rasped.

Rhys opened his eyes and smiled faintly at Wade, his sweat-slicked chest heaving with his pants. "Yeah?"

Wade grunted and rubbed his nose against Rhys's. "Hell yes. Was that one of your fantasies too?"

Rhys hesitated before nodding wordlessly, his expression suddenly shy.

Shit. He's so fucking adorable.

Wade lowered his hands to Rhys's butt. "Hold on to

me," he said gruffly before shuffling to the edge of the bed with Rhys still on his lap.

Rhys gasped, his legs wrapping instinctively around Wade's hips and his fingers flexing on Wade's shoulders as Wade rose and carried him into the en suite bathroom, cock still firmly wedged inside Rhys's ass.

CHAPTER SEVENTEEN

"I'm keeping the baby," Misaki Oshiro said, her knuckles white where she'd laced her hands together atop her crossed knees.

Wade glanced at Rhys. The latter stood leaning against the desk beside him, his baby blue eyes steady as he looked at Misaki.

Although Rhys's expression remained neutral, Wade could tell he was relieved at hearing Misaki's decision. It amazed Wade how much better he could read Rhys now that they were sleeping with each other.

Two weeks had passed since that fateful weekend when they first had sex. And with every passing day, Wade unravelled yet another facet of Rhys he hadn't known before. Like how fussy he'd become about his morning routine. Or how he liked to organize his wardrobe and bathroom toiletries just so.

Wade bit back a wry smile. *Although that shouldn't really surprise me. It's scary how much of a stickler for perfection he's been since our college days.*

Wade caught Misaki looking curiously between Rhys and him. He cleared his throat and dipped his chin at the nervous woman seated across from them. "I'm glad to hear that."

Misaki sighed, her shoulders relaxing. She pursed her lips and gazed from Wade to Rhys. "So, you're not disappointed?"

Rhys grimaced. "Why the hell would we be disappointed? We're not your parents."

Wade studied Misaki with a sympathetic expression. "By the way, what *did* you tell them?"

Wade and Rhys had met the senior Oshiros at one of the annual office family gatherings. Misaki's parents were pretty straight-laced and seemed the type to collapse from shock at the news that their one and only daughter intended to have a baby out of wedlock.

Misaki pulled a face. "The truth. It was a disaster. I seriously thought they were going to disown me. They were mollified to an extent when I told them about Itsuki."

Wade smiled drily. "I bet they were."

Although Itsuki Yamazaki looked like a baby-faced brat who hadn't started shaving yet, he was twenty-five years old and the only heir to the Yamazaki group, a chain of restaurants that had started life as a small mom and pop store and now catered for businesses across Tokyo, Nagoya, and as far south as Kyoto and Osaka. Like his father before him, Itsuki was working his way up the corporate ladder from the very bottom while doing a degree at a renowned business school in Tokyo.

"How are things between you and Itsuki?" Rhys said.

Misaki's face relaxed in a soft smile. "To be honest, not as bad as I thought they would be. He's not worried about our ten-year age gap and he's excited about the baby. He's insisted on coming to all the prenatal appointments with me." She sighed again. "He's even talking about weddings and stuff, but it's too early for that yet. We're just getting to know each other."

"I'm glad things have worked out okay," Wade said. "We need to get you in with human resources to sort out your maternity leave and pay."

Misaki nodded and looked from Wade to Rhys again. "I want to come back to work," she said, her tone firm. "Tomorrow, if that's okay."

Rhys raised an eyebrow. "You sure?"

Misaki smiled. "I'm pregnant, not sick." Her face fell slightly. "Although I gotta admit morning sickness is still a bitch. I might dash off to the restroom from time to time." She wrinkled her nose. "God, even the thought of pickled herring makes me want to hurl these days."

It wasn't until evening that Wade got Rhys to himself again. It was gone seven by the time Wade logged off his computer, rose from his desk, and strolled across the open-plan floor space to the corridor that led to Rhys's room. They were the last ones left in the building. Even Gabe, who usually stayed late, had disappeared an hour ago to go meet with his wedding planner.

Wade propped his shoulder against the doorframe

of Rhys's office and watched Rhys shrug into his suit jacket where he stood looking through a panoramic wall to the dazzling lights of the city spread out below, his back to Wade. Rhys had picked a large room at the far end of their corner plot on the twentieth floor of the glass-and-steel building that housed the Tokyo branch of their business.

"You ready?" Wade said.

Rhys startled and twisted on his heels. His lips curved in a small smile, but not before Wade glimpsed the anxious light in his eyes.

Wade stiffened slightly where he stood in the doorway. "What's wrong, Rhys?"

Surprise flashed across Rhys's face for a second. He evidently thought he'd successfully masked whatever was troubling him.

"Nothing," Rhys mumbled.

Irritation darted through Wade. It irked him that Rhys still didn't feel completely comfortable sharing his most private thoughts with him. "It's something, Rhys." Wade walked into the room and closed the door. "We're not leaving here until you tell me what it is," he continued in a hard voice.

Rhys gazed silently at him before running a hand through his hair and sighing. "With Misaki coming back to work, we're not going to be needed as much for the Osaka project."

Understanding dawned in Wade's mind. He frowned. "So what? Are you saying our proposition no longer stands?"

"I—," Rhys hesitated and swallowed, his gaze

dropping to the floor, " —I'm game, but only if you still want to."

Wade stared at the faint color staining Rhys's cheeks.

God, he's the most sexy, pig-headed, infuriating bastard I've ever known!

Wade knew he had his work cut out for him when he'd suggested their crazy proposition four weeks ago.

Shit, has it really been four weeks?

What he hadn't anticipated was how hard Rhys would fight him at every step. And how terrified Rhys still appeared to be deep inside at what was happening between them.

"Considering that we've fucked literally every night for the last eighteen days, I think you can safely assume that it's still game on, Rhys," Wade said silkily. He twisted the lock on the door and turned to face Rhys.

Rhys's eyes widened. "Why did you—" He drew a breath in sharply when Wade reached out to the wall and flicked the light switch.

CHAPTER EIGHTEEN

Darkness descended around them, the only illumination coming from the brightly lit, colorful city beyond the dual aspect glass walls.

"Why did I turn off the light?" Wade said. He took a step toward Rhys and felt a thrill shoot through him when Rhys stepped back. Wade knew Rhys wasn't afraid of him physically. He could tell from Rhys's expression in the ambient glow bathing the office that this, whatever Wade was intending, excited him as much as it intrigued him.

"We've played out several of the fuck fantasies you've had about me," Wade said silkily as he walked toward Rhys, the filthy idea he'd been dreaming of since the beginning of the week crystallizing into a sudden craving that made his cock harden in a handful of seconds. "Pretty loudly and eloquently at times, I might add. I think we should fulfill one of mine."

Rhys backed away from Wade until there was nowhere left to go, his cheeks flaming in the vibrant lighting at Wade's taunting words while he stood against the glass facade.

Wade's dick throbbed as he placed his hands on the transparent wall on either side of Rhys's head and caged him in. Rhys's breaths washed across Wade's throat, sharp and fast. His blue eyes glittered in the gloom as he tilted his chin and looked up at Wade.

"It's time I showed you just how serious I am about our…proposition, Rhys," Wade hissed. He dipped his head and tugged on Rhys's left earlobe with his teeth.

Rhys shivered, a low moan rumbling out of his throat. He gasped when Wade grabbed his waist and twisted him around to face the glass wall. Wade gripped Rhys's hands where he'd placed them on the cool surface for support.

"In fact, I think you deserve a punishment for even doubting the seriousness of my intentions," Wade growled in Rhys's right ear, his hands dropping to palm Rhys's ass.

Rhys groaned and lowered his hands from the glass.

"No!" Wade barked, grasping Rhys's hands and placing them back on the wall. "Keep your hands on the glass, Rhys." Wade punched his hips forward and pressed his erection against the crack of Rhys's butt. "You don't get to touch me for this."

Rhys shuddered and arched his ass against Wade's cock. He spread his fingers and held on to the wall, his pants loud above the distant sound of traffic from the city below.

Blood pounded in Wade's veins and dick as he reached

around Rhys's waist and unbuckled his pants. Rhys stiffened when Wade slid the zipper down and hooked his thumbs in the waistband of his trousers and briefs.

"Wade," Rhys mumbled nervously, his fingers curling on the glass.

"Don't worry," Wade murmured. He nibbled the top of Rhys's right ear. "They can't see us."

A cluster of high-rises rose on the other side of the streets framing the busy intersection where their building stood. Lights still shone brightly on most of the floors, and office workers were visible behind the glass windows and walls.

Rhys cursed when Wade yanked his trousers and briefs down to his ankles, exposing his erect, leaking cock.

"That's nice," Wade said throatily, peering around Rhys. He reached his left hand out and trailed the back of his knuckles up and down Rhys's trembling shaft. "Let's see if we can't make you...wetter."

Wade clutched Rhys's hips in his hands and pulled him back several steps until he leaned forward at the waist, his upper body angled toward the wall and his hands flat on the glass.

"What a nice view," Wade purred, his hungry gaze roaming Rhys's body all the way from the enticing curve of his neck down to his naked butt cheeks and strong thighs. "You're so fucking sexy, Rhys. Let me show you just how much you drive me crazy."

With that, Wade dropped to his knees, tugged on Rhys's ankles to spread his legs wide, parted Rhys's crack with his hands, and flicked his tongue against Rhys's hole.

"*Wade!*" Rhys cried out, shivering violently in Wade's strong grip. His palms squeaked against the glass as his hands slipped an inch.

"I told you not to move, Rhys," Wade growled, nipping Rhys's left butt cheek with his teeth.

Rhys froze above him, breaths shuddering loudly out of his lungs while his knuckles whitened on the glass, fixing his hands to the cool facade.

"There you go," Wade murmured, his cock pushing painfully against the zipper of his pants as he kissed the mark he'd made on Rhys's skin. "I think you deserve a reward for that."

Wade took a firm hold of Rhys's ass and started licking and sucking his hole in earnest, his senses drowning in Rhys's intoxicating scent and sinful taste. Rimming was something Wade had only occasionally indulged in in the past. He'd become an ardent fan of the sexy practice since he'd started sleeping with Rhys. And it wasn't just because he got such a kick out of driving Rhys wild when he did it to him. Wade was surprised to discover that stimulating Rhys so intimately stirred him up just as badly.

Rhys's moans and gasps echoed in the gloom around them as Wade pleasured him. A shocked cry erupted from Rhys when Wade furrowed his stiff tongue and poked the tip through Rhys's twitching folds. Wade groaned as he stabbed and circled the taut, sensitive rim, desire sending his heart slamming against his ribs while Rhys practically shouted out in pleasure.

Wade could tell from Rhys's tense body that he was close to climaxing. He reached his left hand between Rhys's thighs and palmed Rhys's hot, quivering cock from below while he continued tonguing his hole.

"*Fuck!*" Rhys yelled out, his hands fisting on the glass facade.

Wade matched the rhythm of his probing tongue and that of his fingers on Rhys's throbbing shaft. All it took was a few wicked strokes inside Rhys's spasming hole and on his jerking cock for him to explode in Wade's hands.

Rhys's breathing froze for a timeless moment before he hiccuped and came violently, his entire body tightening like a bow while he filled Wade's hand with his hot cum.

Wade unbuckled his trousers hurriedly, yanked his zipper and briefs down to free his painful dick, and rose to his feet, lust a red haze that filled his vision. He coated the broad head of his cock and his shaft with Rhys's cum before rubbing Rhys's hole with his sticky fingers, Rhys's musky scent filling the space between them.

Rhys grunted when Wade pushed two fingers inside him and scissored them, stretching his already soft entrance. Wade yanked his fingers out of Rhys's passage, guided his cock to Rhys's opening, and entered Rhys in a single, savage thrust that had Rhys crying out and rising on his toes.

Wade grabbed Rhys's waist in a punishing grip and

started pounding Rhys's ass, his hips rolling powerfully and his balls slamming against Rhys's butt cheeks. Rhys rocked back and forth on his feet, arms straining for support against the glass, his cries dropping to muffled groans as he sank his teeth into the sleeve of his right forearm.

Wade moved one hand to the crown of Rhys's head and curled his fingers in the thick blond strands before tugging on them. Rhys's voice rose again as his neck arched up and back, his spine bowing beautifully under Wade's hot gaze.

Wade leaned forward and brought his lips to Rhys's right ear. "That's it," he hissed. "Let me hear you scream, Rhys."

And Rhys did just that as Wade fucked him harder and faster until he came all over the glass wall while Wade ejaculated deep inside his hole, the vibrant lights of the city bathing them in a colorful glow.

CHAPTER NINETEEN

"You're hot."

Rhys stifled a smile as he observed Wade's response to Ethan Skye's blunt words.

Wade arched an eyebrow at the blond bartender. "Thanks. You're quite…appealing yourself."

Ethan's face fell. "Appealing?" he repeated, disbelief coloring his voice.

Wade looked at Rhys, unfazed. "Was that the wrong thing to say?"

Ethan sighed and stared between Wade and Rhys. "My ego is crushed. I've been called many things in my life. Cute. Sexy. Hot. Drop-dead, come-in-your-pants gorgeous. But never—," Ethan grimaced, "—appealing."

Rhys chuckled and saw his amusement reflected in Wade's eyes.

Rhys hadn't been sure how Wade would react when he'd suggested coming to *Saron* for a drink. To Rhys's surprise, Wade had seemed curious to return to the place.

"It's somewhere you seem to go often," Wade explained at Rhys's expression. "Of course I'd be interested in finding out more about it."

Despite Rhys's misgivings about where this tryst of theirs was headed, he hadn't been able to crush the thrill that flashed through him at Wade's words. The fact that Wade was actively trying to explore a side of Rhys's life he hadn't known before meant a lot more to Rhys than he'd realized.

Three days had passed since Wade had indulged in one of his own fuck fantasies about Rhys and taken him bareback in their office. The memory of that night was forever etched in Rhys's mind as one of the most sinfully arousing things he had ever done.

Or had done to me, to be precise.

Rhys was distracted from his torrid thoughts by a familiar voice.

"Rhys," someone murmured behind him.

Rhys twisted on the bar stool and looked at the man who'd entered the club and come to a stop beside him. He smiled warmly at Joe Cavendish, the owner of *Saron* and Ethan's boyfriend.

"Joe."

Joe glanced at Wade before focusing on Rhys once more. "I haven't seen you in a while."

Rhys could read Joe's unspoken questions in his steady hazel gaze. *Who's this guy? And where's Michael?*

Joe turned and held out a hand to Wade before Rhys could make the introductions.

"Hi. I'm Joe Cavendish, the owner of this club. Welcome to *Saron.*"

A thoughtful expression dawned in Wade's eyes before he shook Joe's hand. "Wade Tucker."

Joe raised an eyebrow, surprise flashing on his face. "As in the other half of Damon & Tucker?"

Wade smiled. "The one and the same."

Joe smiled back. "I'm a fan of your work."

Rhys released the breath he hadn't even realized he was holding. He wasn't sure how he would have reacted if Wade hadn't gotten on with Joe and Ethan. That was when Rhys realized that he wanted, no, *needed* Wade to like his friends. Friends Wade didn't know about but whom Rhys counted as his brothers in arms. Friends who would drop everything and come to Rhys's aid if he was ever in trouble.

"I can see that," Wade drawled. He glanced around *Saron*'s distinctive decor before turning a curious stare on Rhys and Joe. "You'll have to tell me the story of how you two met."

Rhys glanced at Joe, his ears suddenly burning.

There was no way he was ready to admit to Wade how he'd picked up Joe at *Le Secret*, the internationally renowned upscale escort service, a few years ago in New York. Or how the two men had gone on to have a torrid on-off affair for the next fourteen months. Neither of them had been keen to enter into a relationship, but both of them liked their sex hot and dirty and their bodies had been highly compatible. They'd parted ways amicably when Joe had left the States for Tokyo and reconnected again a couple of years later, after Joe approached Rhys for his help in designing the club he intended to open.

Despite Joe's protests, Rhys had done the job pro bono. In exchange, Rhys never had to pay for his or his guests' drinks when he came to the club, a turn of events Rhys was more than pleased with since *Saron* had ended up becoming his favorite place to hang out in Tokyo after he and Wade relocated to Japan.

"Maybe I should let Rhys do the telling," Joe said tactfully as he headed behind the bar.

Ethan watched his boyfriend thoughtfully before leaning across the counter toward Wade.

"Hey, you thinking the same thing as me? That they used to be fuck buddies?" Ethan said in a low voice.

Rhys nearly choked on his Scotch.

Wade dragged his gaze from Rhys's flushed cheeks and observed Ethan steadily. "What makes you think that?"

Rhys didn't miss the way Wade's knuckles whitened slightly on his glass. Surprise flared through him. *Is he jealous?*

Ethan grimaced. "I can sense this vibe between them. Besides—," he cocked a thumb at Rhys, "—this guy likes men with huge junks. And, if you don't mind me saying so, you look like you have an enormous package."

"Excuse me while I have a word with my employee," Joe interrupted in a silky voice. He grabbed Ethan around the waist, lifted him off his feet, and carried him to a dark corner of the bar.

Akihito, one of the other bartenders, watched them with an exasperated expression. "I'm sorry about that," he murmured to Wade. "He has a filter missing."

Wade smiled faintly as he watched Joe crowd Ethan against a drinks shelf and proceed to kiss him senseless.

"They always like this?" he said, glancing curiously at Rhys.

"More often than you think," Rhys drawled, looking at his friends with an amused expression.

"Amen to that," muttered one of the club patrons next to Rhys.

A chorus of agreement echoed along the bar.

"They should just strip and start charging for the sex show," another man said dreamily while Ethan wrapped one leg around Joe's muscular thigh and squeezed his butt cheeks.

It was late by the time Rhys and Wade left *Saron* and reached Rhys's apartment. They headed straight for Rhys's bedroom, Wade's hands on Rhys's waist while he kissed and nibbled on Rhys's neck.

Rhys shivered and bit back a groan.

Seriously, where does he get the energy from?

Although he'd been tired at the start of the evening, Rhys's own fatigue had faded at Wade's first kiss and his touch, as it always did.

He truly is a magician.

Wade stepped away from Rhys, kicked off his shoes, and slipped his tie free from the collar of his shirt. Rhys walked across to him and took the necktie from his grip. Wade looked at him, puzzled. His lips curved in an amused smile when Rhys wrapped the scarlet strip around his left wrist.

"What are you doing?" Wade murmured, examining the material knotted on his skin.

Rhys flashed him an arrogant smirk and cocked an eyebrow. "I'm about to fulfill one of your other fantasies."

Wade's eyes darkened. He stepped up to Rhys and trailed his left hand down Rhys's right cheek, the silk tie fluttering at his wrist. "Oh yeah?"

"Yes," Rhys said, closing his eyes briefly at the sensual caress.

It didn't matter how many times Wade had touched him since the night he first stormed into *Saron* and dragged him home. A graze of Wade's fingers. A stroke of his palm. That was all it took to ignite Rhys's skin.

CHAPTER TWENTY

WADE SHUDDERED AT THE PASSIONATE LIGHT IN RHYS'S eyes when the latter blinked them open. Rhys raised his hands and lowered Wade's fingers from his face.

"There's only one condition," Rhys said. "You're not allowed to touch me."

Wade stared, his pulse spiking at Rhys's command. "Is this payback for the other night?"

Rhys chuckled. The sound danced down Wade's spine and made his dick swell.

"Nope," Rhys drawled. "I think you'll enjoy this better if you just…watch."

Anticipation swirled through Wade as Rhys guided him to climb on the bed and sit at the top end. Rhys slipped his tie from the collar of his shirt and fastened it around Wade's right wrist. He straddled Wade's body and flashed him a sensual smile as he secured the make-shift straps to the posts framing the headboard.

"I think this will do," Rhys murmured, tugging on the silk bands.

"Uh-huh," Wade mumbled, his attention focused on where Rhys's crotch touched the tent of Wade's splendid erection. He bit back a groan when Rhys shuffled off the end of the bed.

Rhys stood and moved back a few steps. He paused, placed his hands on his hips, and tilted his head to the side while he stared at Wade, admiring his handy work.

"I could get used to this," Rhys said. "Now, stay."

Rhys's hands rose to the buttons of his shirt. He undid them one by one, his movements slow and seductive, his heated gaze locked on Wade's.

Wade swallowed. *He's going to drive me insane.*

By the time Rhys finished the most raunchy striptease Wade had ever been treated to in his entire adult life, Wade was so hard his dick throbbed painfully behind the zipper of his pants.

Rhys glanced at Wade's groin and bit his lip. "Hmm," he hummed. "I can't wait to get that inside me."

"Shit," Wade groaned, hips punching up at Rhys's filthy words.

"But first, my hole is hungry for something else," Rhys added mysteriously.

Wade frowned when Rhys walked around to the nightstand by the right side of the bed, took the lube out of the top drawer, and opened the bottom compartment.

Holy. Fuck.

Wade's fingers curled on the silk bands holding him prisoner as he stared at the object Rhys had removed from the drawer.

It was the dildo he had seen Rhys use on himself that first night he discovered Rhys wanted him.

Rhys cocked an eyebrow at Wade. "Remember this?"

Wade nodded wordlessly, too aroused to speak.

Rhys smiled as he stroked the large, flesh-colored sex toy with his fingers, his gaze growing hooded. "I haven't used this since we started sleeping with each other. I seem to recall you saying you liked watching me—," he paused and licked his lips in an alluring move that had Wade's hips rising off the bed again in a reflexive thrust, "—what was it again? Oh, yeah. *Driving it up my ass*, I believe were your exact words."

"*Fuck*, Rhys!" Wade swore, his body so hot he was surprised he hadn't scorched the bedsheets.

Rhys shuddered and reached down to stroke his hard, leaking cock. "Oh, I'm going to, Wade. And you're gonna watch while I do it."

Wade's heart slammed against his ribs so hard he thought he was having a coronary.

Rhys dropped the lube and the dildo on the bed, and climbed on the mattress. He faced Wade, spread Wade's legs wide open, and squatted between them, just far enough back for Wade to get a full-frontal view of Rhys's entire body.

The snap of the bottle lid opening was loud in the charged silence that filled the bedroom.

Wade clenched his jaw as Rhys poured a generous amount of lube in his right hand, coated the dildo liberally with the liquid, and set it back down on the bed. Rhys spread his thighs wide open, dropped his left hand on the mattress behind his back so he leaned slightly away from Wade, and brought his wet fingers to his hole.

A low moan rumbled out of Rhys as he rubbed his pink entrance. Wade shivered at the sexy sound, his eyes locked on Rhys's fingers where he played with himself. Wade groaned when Rhys slipped one finger, then two inside himself, his passage opening deliciously to swallow his digits to the last knuckle.

Rhys trembled and panted while he finger fucked himself, the muscles in his strong thighs moving sinuously as he started jacking his hips up and down, his stiff cock bobbing in a matching cadence.

He rode his hand for a full minute before slipping his fingers out of his slick opening, sweat beading his face and chest, his lips swollen where he'd chewed them.

Wade's chest heaved, his breathing accelerating with his growing arousal. He gripped the ties binding him when Rhys reached for the dildo and rose up on his heels to line the thick head with his hole.

They had indulged in plenty of titillating play in the month they'd been seeing each other but this, *this* right here, was going to go down in the annals of their history as one of the single most electrifying sexual act Rhys had ever performed for him.

As if sensing Wade's thoughts, Rhys moaned his name in a sultry voice that sent a shiver of pure need down Wade's spine.

"Wade."

Then Rhys slowly impaled himself on the dildo, his

head dropping backward and his entire body stiffening as he stuffed himself with the thick love stick in a single, languid thrust.

Wade gnashed his teeth as he watched Rhys rise up off the dildo before going down on it again, the folds of his passage stretched wide and dragging the rim of tight muscles guarding his opening along the slick, latex surface.

Rhys's lips parted on increasingly savage cries and moans as he fucked himself with his favorite toy, his wrist twisting and angling the stout shaft to hit his prostate as he drove it harder and faster inside himself, his toes curling in the bedsheets.

In that moment, Wade thought he had never seen anything as erotic as Rhys pleasuring himself in such a disinhibited and decadent fashion.

That's it!

Wade growled, stretched his body to the right, and maneuvered the loop of the tie holding his wrist captive up and off the bed post. He freed his left hand in the next second, rose to his knees on the bed, and pushed Rhys down on the mattress in front of him.

RHYS GASPED AS HE LANDED ON HIS BACK, THE CROOK OF his knees finding Wade's hips. The fire in Wade's slate-blue eyes threatened to burn Rhys alive as he towered over him, Wade's left hand heavy where he pressed down on Rhys's trembling abdomen.

Rhys whimpered when Wade wrapped his right

hand on his fingers on the handle of the dildo. Wade stared into Rhys's feverish gaze, yanked the love stick out, and shoved it back inside Rhys's body to the hilt.

Rhys cried out and let go of the toy, his fingers finding the top of Wade's thighs. Tortured moans and gasps ripped out of him as Wade took control of the dildo and drove it repeatedly in and out of his tingling, sensitive passage.

"Fuck!" Wade snarled, working Rhys's hole harder and faster with the sex toy and nudging his prostate over and over again with the broad head.

Rhys bit down hard on his lower lip as intense pleasure sent flashes of light pulsing across his vision.

Electricity shot up Rhys's spine as the first wave of his climax spiraled through him. A band of pressure built up deep inside his lower belly, tightening his balls and making his passage spasm around the thick dildo. Rhys's eyes widened, his pulse skittering at the shocking, intense sensation.

A guttural shout tore out of Rhys when his orgasm slammed into him with the force of a hurricane. His mind went white as he arched his head back into the mattress and stared blindly at the ceiling. A buzzing sound filled his ears while fierce waves of ecstasy started throbbing through him. Rhys grasped Wade's thighs in a punishing grip as his legs straightened out stiffly on either side of Wade's hips. His breath locked in his throat. He bowed his spine off the bed and curled his toes in the air, his body drowning in the most earth-shattering pleasure.

Rhys realized dimly he must have blanked out a

little at some point as the next thing he knew, Wade had replaced the dildo with his hot cock and was pounding Rhys's ass with savage grunts, his face contorted in a fierce snarl. Rhys shivered and surrendered his limp, pliant body to Wade while the latter hooked his hands under Rhys's knees and pushed Rhys's legs up in the air. It didn't take long for Rhys's spent cock to stir against his belly and swell with fresh arousal at the forceful way Wade was taking him.

Wade cursed when his gaze dropped to Rhys's erection. He pressed Rhys's legs higher and bowed his head and body, his hips still thrusting his cock deep and hard inside Rhys, his movements untamed.

Rhys nearly screamed when Wade wrapped his lips and tongue around the head of his dick and sucked him once, then twice.

An animal sound left Wade, as if the taste of Rhys was his final undoing.

The bed rocked as Wade accelerated the pace of his rolling hips and fucked Rhys to within an inch of his life. White noise filled Rhys's world when they found their release together, Rhys's cock jerking his hot cum all over his chest and neck while Wade poured his own seed deep inside Rhys's body, making a sticky mess of the both of them.

CHAPTER TWENTY-ONE

"Fancy going to *Saron* for a drink?" Rhys said, leaning against the doorframe of Wade's office.

It was the end of the week leading up to Christmas. Most of the staff had left early for the long holiday weekend.

Wade rubbed a hand across the back of his head and flashed a tired smile at Rhys. "I wish I could, but something's come up. A prospective client called and wants to meet. She's only in town for one night."

Rhys arched an eyebrow, curious. "Anyone I know?"

Wade leaned back in his chair. "You've probably heard of her. Lana Keele, the president of Keele Industries?"

The name Keele was one Rhys was familiar with. A conglomerate that used to feature regularly in the Forbes's top one hundred list of companies, it had been in steady decline until a sudden revival five years ago, when Lana Keele, the only child of the company's founder George Keele, finally took over the family business.

"You'll have to tell me how it goes," Rhys murmured.

Wade dipped his chin. "I'll come over to yours after." He hesitated. "You still going to *Saron?*"

"Uh-huh," Rhys said. He smiled at Wade's scowl. "What, you don't trust me?"

"It's not you I don't trust," Wade grumbled. "It's the sharks circling around you every time we go there that I'm worried about."

Rhys laughed and pushed off the doorway. "I'll see you back at my place," he said over his shoulder as he headed to his office.

"Don't do anything I wouldn't do," Wade called out.

Two hours and one Scotch later, and Rhys was ready to leave the club.

"You going already?" Joe said from the other side of the counter as Rhys slipped off the barstool.

Rhys smiled. "Yup. Got a hot date."

He'd texted Wade a while back to tell him he was making his way to the apartment and had received a reply from Wade that he wouldn't be long.

Ethan grinned at Rhys, his green eyes sparkling with amusement.

"What?" Rhys said suspiciously.

"Nothing," Ethan said. "It's just, I've never seen you this happy before. It suits you better than the prissy look you normally wear."

Rhys stuck his middle finger up at Ethan.

"And now the asshole is back," Ethan groaned while Joe chuckled.

Rhys was almost at the entrance when Michael walked through the doors. They froze and stared at each other awkwardly for a moment.

"Umm, hi," Rhys murmured, a spasm of guilt shooting through him as he recalled their last conversation.

Michael let out a sigh. "Seriously, stop looking at me as if you expect me to punch you."

"Sorry," Rhys mumbled. He couldn't see any trace of accusation in Michael's eyes, something he was grateful for.

"You going already?" Michael said, watching Rhys take his coat off the attendant. He looked past Rhys, his gaze roaming the dim interior of the club.

"Wade isn't with me, if that's who you're looking for," Rhys said drily.

Michael inhaled sharply. "He—he *dumped* you already?!"

Rhys narrowed his eyes. "I'm going to choose to ignore that comment. No, he had a business meeting. And yes, before you ask, we're still seeing each other."

"Oh," Michael grunted. He grimaced and ran a hand through his hair. "Well, you can't blame a man for hoping."

Remorse stabbed through Rhys once more. "I—I'm—"

"Don't," Michael said gruffly. "Don't apologize. I can see in your eyes when you talk about him how happy you are."

Rhys blinked, startled. "You're the second person who's said that tonight. Is it that obvious?"

Michael smiled ruefully. "Only to those who know you well." He glanced toward the interior of the club and hesitated. "Mind if I walk you out?"

Rhys smiled faintly. "Sure. If you promise to be a gentleman and leave my virtue intact."

Michael chuckled. "I solemnly swear not to lose control of my manly urges and paw you."

Rhys laughed as they headed out of the club. They chatted amiably while they walked toward the main Shinjuku strip.

"Well, this is my stop," Rhys said, shoving his hands in the pockets of his coat as they slowed by a taxi stand.

"It was good to see you again," Michael murmured. "Seriously, you look great. And I say that as a friend."

"Thanks," Rhys said gratefully. "Maybe one day, we could go for a drink, you, me, and Wade?"

Michael grunted, his gaze shifting past Rhys. "I honestly don't think that's such a great—" He froze, his eyes widening as he stared at something.

"Michael?" Rhys said, puzzled. He twisted on his heels and followed Michael's gaze to the other side of a busy intersection.

A bus trundled past just then, obscuring Rhys's view of whatever it was that had captured Michael's attention. "What is it?" he murmured, glancing at Michael.

Michael startled and looked at Rhys, his expression pained. "Shit. Rhys, I—"

The bus disappeared down the noisy strip and Rhys got his first view of what had transfixed Michael.

Wade and a brunette in a green cocktail dress stood on the steps of an exclusive restaurant. The woman had her back to the road and was clutching Wade's broad shoulders while Wade leaned down, one hand on the woman's waist while the other touched her face. He said something with a smile. From the way the woman's shoulders shook, she'd laughed at whatever it was Wade had murmured to her.

Rhys was dimly aware that Michael was calling his name and talking to him. He felt Michael's hand land on his shoulder and wondered vaguely why his touch felt so fuzzy. His next thought was that it didn't matter. Nothing mattered anymore.

In that moment, Rhys felt his entire world spin to a stop before slowly crumbling around him. It wasn't until his vision blurred that he realized he was crying.

Rhys continued staring at the indistinct figures across the street for a timeless moment. A gasp left his lips when someone grabbed his shoulders and twisted him around forcefully.

Rhys blinked and looked up into Michael's anxious face, the lawyer's voice finally penetrating the heavy fog paralyzing his senses.

"Rhys, get a grip of yourself!" Michael barked. He glanced across the street, anger flashing in his eyes. "He—"

"Take me," Rhys whispered between numb lips. "Take me somewhere."

"What?" Michael blinked, confusion washing across his face. "Do you want me to bring you back to your—"

"*No!* Not—not there. He—," Rhys closed his eyes and swallowed the hard lump in his throat, "—he said he was coming over after."

Michael studied Rhys for a moment before gently taking him in his arms. "Hush," he murmured in Rhys's hair while Rhys's tears soaked his shirt. "It's going to be okay. You're going to be okay."

Rhys closed his eyes and fisted his hands in Michael's coat, knowing the lawyer's words were a lie.

He would never be alright. Not for as long as he lived.

CHAPTER TWENTY-TWO

"Seriously, I'm so sorry," Lana Keele said, her cheeks flushed with embarrassment. She blinked and touched her left eye where Wade had just slipped her contact lens back in.

Wade smiled, his hand dropping from Lana's waist. "I hope you don't take offense, but you're nothing like what I imagined you would be."

Lana's face fell so comically that Wade couldn't help chuckling.

The restaurant door opened and closed behind Wade. Someone paused on the top step and sighed. It was a long suffering sound, as if the person who'd made it did so on a daily basis. Wade looked over his shoulder and met the sardonic stare of Tom Sutherland, Lana's secretary-cum-assistant-cum-personal slave.

"What happened?" the dark-eyed man drawled. He was holding their coats in his arms. "Did she jump you?"

Wade didn't miss the faint undertone of jealousy that underscored Sutherland's voice. He'd seen the way Lana's secretary had sometimes looked at her while they were having dinner and discussing the business proposition they'd approached Wade with. From Lana's demeanor, it was clear she was blissfully unaware that Sutherland was in love with her, and in a bad way at that.

"Hey, I'm standing right here!" Lana snapped, her green eyes full of indignation. "It's those darn new contacts. One of them fell out and Wade was helping me put it back in!"

"I told you you should stick to specs," Tom said. "They make you look more business-like and less—," his gaze roamed Lana's body from the top of her artfully made hair, all the way down to her expensive high heels, "—femme fatale. Besides, you should accept the fact that you're growing old gracefully. Myopia isn't anything to be ashamed of."

Wade bit the inside of his cheek to stop the laughter threatening to burst out of him as Lana opened and closed her mouth soundlessly, too shocked for words. He'd rarely seen two people more suited for one another than this pair and he hoped Lana realized it and soon, before Tom's rigid self-control snapped.

"You asshole!" Lana hissed.

"Right back at you, sweetheart," Tom retorted. He handed Wade his coat, shrugged into his own jacket, and walked down the steps to drop Lana's overcoat around her shoulders. "Now, let's get out of here and let this poor man go back to his lover." He grabbed

Lana's hand and started guiding her along the curb. "Goodnight, Mr. Tucker. I'll be in touch soon to finalize the contract."

"Bye, Wade," Lana grumbled over her shoulder. "Hey, what makes you think he has a lover?" she hissed at Tom as they walked off into the night.

"Because you flirted with him for the first five minutes of our meeting and he didn't bat an eyelid," Tom replied. "On the other hand, this could also mean you're losing your touch. Maybe we need to work on your sex appeal."

Wade grinned and shook his head as he watched the pair continue to bicker while they disappeared among the busy evening crowd. He could tell he was going to like working with them.

Rhys is gonna laugh when I tell him about tonight.

With that thought in mind, Wade crossed the road and got inside a waiting cab, suddenly impatient to see his lover.

Rhys's apartment was dark when Wade entered it twenty minutes later.

He frowned, puzzled. *Maybe he's in bed already.* A wry grimace curved Wade's lips in the next instant. *Well, we* have *fucked every single day this week, so he's probably exhausted. I should try and abstain tonight.*

The first thread of unease unfolded inside Wade when he reached Rhys's room and saw the empty bed.

"Rhys?" Wade called out, his gaze shifting to the en suite bathroom.

It was just as empty and dark as the rest of the apartment.

Wade slipped his cell out of his pocket and checked his messages. Almost an hour had passed since Rhys had texted to say he was leaving *Saron*.

Where is he?

Wade headed back into the lounge, poured himself a drink from the bar, and sat on the suede couch where he'd first given Rhys a hand job. Although he told himself he was being paranoid and that there were a dozen possible explanations for why Rhys could be late, Wade couldn't help his growing apprehension. Something felt off. He couldn't put a finger on why he thought that but he just sensed it, deep in the most primitive part of his mind.

By the time dawn peeked pale fingers above the horizon, Wade was close to losing his mind. Rhys hadn't come home, nor had he replied to any of Wade's messages and calls. Wade paced Rhys's lounge for the umpteenth time while he considered his options. He'd already checked the local news for accidents and rang all the hospitals in the area to see if someone fitting Rhys's description had been brought in as a patient. Although he was sorely tempted to call the cops, Wade knew they wouldn't be interested until Rhys had been missing for over twenty-four hours.

He was wearing a thin thread in Rhys's floorboards when his cell suddenly dinged across the room. Wade strode over to the couch, snatched up his phone, and swore when he fumbled it.

His heart raced in his chest as he frantically scanned the screen.

A text had come through. It was from Rhys.

A dull roar filled Wade's ears when he read the message.

TWELVE HOURS LATER, WADE FOUND HIMSELF IN FRONT of a condominium in mid town. He glared up at the facade of the building, clenched his jaw, and headed inside.

Michael Lynch's apartment was on the eighth floor of the tower. He opened the door at Wade's insistent banging and swore when Wade barged past him and stormed inside the place.

"Where is he?" Wade snapped, his gaze roaming the open plan lounge and kitchen diner spread out before him.

"Where's who?" Michael retorted harshly.

Wade whirled around and stared at the man glowering at him from the entrance hall of his apartment.

"Rhys. Where is he?" Wade said between gritted teeth, barely holding on to his anger.

He couldn't see any sign of Rhys, nor could he smell Rhys's cologne and his unique scent.

Wade had spent most of the day waiting outside *Saron* for Joe and Ethan to come open up the club. When he'd told them about Rhys going missing and the bewildering text he'd received that morning, Ethan had stared blindly at Wade before glancing at Joe, concern clouding his green eyes.

"I think I saw him leave with Michael last night,"

Ethan said quietly. "It looked like they bumped into each other in the foyer."

Joe's eyes widened while Wade's stomach sank at this news.

Wade knew Rhys wasn't the type to cheat on him. There had to be another explanation for the insane message Rhys had sent him that morning. And it seemed Rhys's former lover was the only lead Wade had to go on.

Joe and Ethan had spent the next hour phoning their contacts to obtain Lynch's address. Although Wade's own nerves were frazzled after the hellish night and day he had just lived through, he was grateful for the two men's help.

Rhys had great friends and Wade intended to tell him that the next time he saw him.

"Let us know if you find out anything," Joe called out to Wade as the latter hurriedly left the club, Lynch's address in hand. "And whatever that message is about, fix it."

Wade had nodded at Joe's grim expression before heading out into the night and hailing a cab.

"I know you were with Rhys last night," Wade said presently to the man whose apartment he was trespassing upon. "Ethan said he saw you two leave the club together."

Michael slammed his front door shut and crossed the floor to the edge of the lounge. They scowled at each other across the space for several seconds.

"I really don't see what Rhys saw in you," Michael said finally with a derisive bark.

Wade narrowed his eyes at the past tense. "That's none of your business now, is it?"

"It is after the way you fucked up last night!" Michael roared.

Wade's heart stuttered. "What do you mean by that?" he said in a deadly tone.

Michael's hands curled into fists. "We saw you. With that woman."

Wade blinked. "Lana Keele?" he said with a faint frown. "We were having a business dinner. Rhys knew about it."

Michael sneered. "Do you kiss all the women you do business with?"

Wade rocked back on his heels, stunned. "I didn't kiss her! Why the hell would you think that?"

Michael folded his arms across his chest, his expression accusing. "The way you were holding her and touching her made it pretty clear that you weren't far off from doing so."

Dread filled Wade as he recalled the incident on the steps of the restaurant. To anyone else watching that scene unfold, it would have been natural to conclude that Lana and him were an item.

Shit. Is that what Rhys thought too?

Wade tasted ash in his mouth as he finally grasped the context of Rhys's message that morning.

"Where is he?" he said quietly.

Michael shook his head, disbelief washing across his face. "You are unreal. What the hell makes you think I would tell you his whereabouts?"

Wade's pulse jumped.

So he knows where Rhys is!

Wade closed the distance to Michael and grabbed the front of the lawyer's T-shirt. "Because I didn't cheat on him," he grated out, a muscle jumping in his cheek. "I was helping Lana put her contact lens back in. And if you guys had waited another half minute, you would have seen her secretary come out and take her back to their hotel."

Michael's eyes widened. "Are you serious?"

"As a heart attack," Wade grunted. He released his hold on Michael's T-shirt. "So, where is he?"

Michael studied him for a moment.

"This thing between you and Rhys," he said, "are you in it half-heartedly? Because if you are—"

"I'm never been more serious about anything or anyone in my entire life," Wade stated curtly.

Michael watched him with a skeptical expression. "But you're straight."

Anger surged through Wade at the lawyer's audacity. He suppressed his fury in the next instant.

The guy's only looking out for Rhys's best interests.

"This isn't about being gay or straight," Wade said steadily.

Michael's expression thawed at whatever he saw on Wade's face. He hesitated before walking across to the coffee table and grabbing a pen and a notepad. He scribbled something on it, tore the top sheet free, and handed it to Wade.

"One of my clients has a holiday rental just outside Nagano," the lawyer said stiffly. "It's a cabin in the mountains. I arranged for Rhys to spend a few days there."

"How—," Wade faltered for a beat, "—how bad was he?"

"He cried," Michael said bluntly.

Wade sucked in air, his heart twisting at the thought of the hell Rhys must have gone through last night.

Michael's eyes softened slightly. "I'm the last person who should be saying this, considering how I feel about Rhys, but—you need to put this right."

Wade swallowed. "I know. And thank you."

Michael blinked. "For what?"

Wade flashed him a tired smile. "For being a good friend to him."

CHAPTER TWENTY-THREE

RHYS RUBBED HIS GRITTY EYES BEFORE GAZING BLINDLY into the flames crackling in the open fire pit opposite the couch he slouched in.

It had gone midnight and snow was falling steadily outside, adding to the pale drifts covering the haunting landscape. Although he was exhausted after the night and day that had just passed, Rhys knew it would be futile to climb into the king-size bed under the eaves of the modern, glass and log wood cabin nestled on the slopes of the mountain.

He'd barely managed a few hours sleep in the last twenty-seven hours.

Rhys didn't remember the exact details of how he had gotten here last night. Michael had packed him an overnight bag at his place before putting him on the bullet train to Nagano. The lawyer had arranged for a cab to pick him up at the other end and bring him to the isolated lodge three miles outside a popular skiing resort.

The cabin's pantry and fridge were fully stocked, courtesy of a local catering company, and Rhys had found fresh toiletries in the en suite bathroom when he'd woken up that morning.

He'd made some toast and eaten half of it, more for the sake of putting something in his empty stomach. It had tasted like ash in his mouth. He'd thrown away the rest and borrowed a pair of boots and a ski jacket he'd discovered in a closet in the foyer before going for a long walk. The cold air had numbed his face and body as he trudged through the snow, his restless mind reliving the events of yesterday and the message he'd finally sent Wade after dozens of texts and missed calls from the latter.

Rhys knew Wade had been going out of his mind with worry from the increasingly desperate tone of his messages and voicemails. For one dizzying moment, Rhys had considered not answering them at all. Then, reality had come crashing down upon him, erasing his selfish impulse. He and Wade were still business partners and Rhys knew he would have to face him at some point in the next week.

Something suddenly flashed in the darkness outside the cabin, distracting Rhys from his glum thoughts. Headlights speared the shadows between the trees visible through the triple aspect, panoramic glass walls wrapping around the building. Rhys frowned as the beams headed steadily up the dirt track before disappearing around the back of the property. He rose from the couch, placed his empty glass of Scotch on the coffee table, and padded barefoot into the foyer, curious as to who it could be at this late hour.

The cabin was set in a hundred acres of private land and the closest neighbor was half a mile away.

Rhys reached the front door just as someone started pounding on it. He twisted the latch, grabbed the handle of the thick, oak pivoting panel, and swung it open. He froze in the next instant.

Wade stood on the porch outside. He was dressed in a sweater and jeans and carried a large overnight bag Rhys recognized as one of his own. Fresh snow flakes melted in Wade's dark hair as he gazed steadily at Rhys.

"Hi," he said quietly, glancing at Michael's oversized clothes where they hung loosely on Rhys's frame.

Rage flooded Rhys. He scowled and started closing the door.

Wade slammed his hand onto it and pushed. "Let me in, Rhys."

"Why?" Rhys snarled. He grunted as he tried to maneuver the door closed. *Fucking strong bastard!* "So you can lie to me?!"

Wade clenched his teeth, shoved at the oak panel with all his strength, and crossed the threshold when Rhys stumbled back a step. He closed the door, dropped the bag, and stood staring at Rhys, his posture stiff and his slate eyes dark with emotion.

Rhys's pulse jumped when he read the anger and agony in the gunmetal depths.

"How did you find me?" Rhys said, a muscle jumping in his cheek. He twisted on his heels and stormed inside the lounge, his footsteps carrying him across the heated oak floor and past the open fire to the see-through wall at the opposite end.

There was motion in the reflection in the glass as Wade slowly followed him inside the airy room.

"Michael told me," Wade said.

Shock reverberated through Rhys at Wade's admission. He turned and stared at the man who had broken his heart, blood pounding in his veins.

He couldn't believe Michael had betrayed him.

"He also told me what happened that night," Wade continued, taking a further step inside the room. "About what you saw." He paused. "Or what you *think* you saw."

Rhys fisted his hands, his nails biting into his palms. "I know what I saw. And trust me, I get the message loud and clear!"

Wade stilled then. "So you meant it?" he said in a low voice devoid of emotion. "What you texted this morning? About being tired of it all? About ending this?"

Wade's eyes glittered despite his aloof tone.

A shiver raced across Rhys's skin at the light burning in the smoky blue depths.

Don't. Don't fall for his lies and excuses.

Rhys straightened to his full height and met Wade's gaze unflinchingly, finally ready to do what he should have done weeks ago. No, what he should have done years ago.

"Yes," Rhys said while his heart shattered all over again. "Why prolong this farce any further? It's clear you were only interested in fucking me for the novelty and you decided to move on when a more interesting prospect came along."

Wade closed the distance between them, took Rhys's face in his hands, and kissed him forcefully.

Rhys gasped, momentarily paralyzed in Wade's grip. Heat flooded his chest and he swallowed the fresh tears threatening to overspill his eyes at the taste of Wade's lips. It took everything Rhys had to push Wade away.

"*No!*" He gritted his teeth at the way his voice trembled. "You don't get to kiss me or touch me, ever again. Not after what you did!"

Wade grabbed Rhys's hands and tugged him into his arms in a tight embrace. Rhys shuddered and closed his stinging eyes, angry at himself for the way his body immediately reacted to Wade's touch.

"Last night, I had dinner with Lana Keele and her secretary Tom Sutherland," Wade said softly. "Lana lost her contact lens when we were coming out of the restaurant, and I helped her put it back in. If you and Michael had stayed another thirty seconds, you would have seen Sutherland come out and take Lana back to their hotel."

Rhys blinked and stiffened. He curled his hands in Wade's sweater.

"You seriously expect me to believe that?" he said, his incredulity reflected in his voice as he looked up at Wade.

"Yes," Wade replied. "And I think you'll be thrilled by the project they want us to take on." He let go of Rhys then and gazed at him steadily.

For the first time that night, Rhys registered the

tiredness in Wade's eyes and the fresh worry lines carved in his brow. His heart raced as the words Wade had spoken echoed in his ears.

"I—," Rhys swallowed convulsively, "—are you telling the truth?"

"Yes," Wade said quietly.

Rhys turned to face the glass wall once more, his mind a jumble of twisted thoughts.

"I've been thinking about everything that's happened between us in the last month long and hard during the drive here," Wade said pensively behind him. He paused. "What are you afraid of, Rhys?"

Rhys trembled when he heard Wade take a step toward him and felt the heat of Wade's body at his back.

"Why were you so ready to give up on us?" Wade added.

Rhys's eyes widened at the bitterness underscoring Wade's voice. He shuddered when Wade slowly trailed his left hand down his left arm.

"Why didn't you want to fight for this?"

Rhys's breath stilled as he stared at the reflection of the man behind him. A tormented expression was etched across Wade's face. Rhys closed his eyes then, unable to bear looking at Wade any longer.

"Because if you reject me—*when* you reject me, it will break me," Rhys whispered tremulously. He gulped air in, on the verge of tears once more.

A charged silence filled the space between them.

"What makes you think I'll reject you?" Wade said quietly.

Rhys opened his eyes, turned, and gazed steadily at Wade, a heavy-hearted smile trembling on his lips.

"Because life isn't a fairy tale, Wade. No gay man can expect the straight man he's lusted after for most of his adult life to turn around and tell him he feels the same way. This—," Rhys waved a hand between Wade and him, "—this attraction. What you're feeling for me right now. It will die a natural death once the novelty of it wears off. There is no happy ever after for us. There was never meant to be. So, let's end this. Right here. Right now." Rhys rubbed a hand across his face. "I'm tired, Wade. And I'd rather we try and get back to a functional working relationship before things get ugly between us."

CHAPTER TWENTY-FOUR

Wade stared at Rhys, a thousand thoughts swirling through his mind while his heart thudded against his ribs.

The expression on Rhys's face. His voice. The words he had just spoken.

They tore through Wade, evoking a hurricane of emotions that threatened to drown him. Chief among them was anger. Anger at himself and anger at Rhys.

"You're such a coward," Wade finally said, his voice quivering.

Rhys's eyes widened.

"You never wanted this to work out. From the very start, you were determined to see us fail," Wade continued, unable to mask his resentment as his voice grew in strength.

"Wade, you're not—" Rhys started in a worn out tone.

"What?" Wade interrupted challengingly. "I'm not

thinking straight? Is that what you were going to say?" He clenched his jaw. "Is that your excuse now?"

Rhys frowned. "I don't understand you. I'm giving you a way out. Why are you fighting this so—"

"*Because I never wanted a way out!*" Wade barked.

Rhys startled.

"I wanted a way in," Wade continued in a tortured voice. "I've always wanted a way into you." He raised his hands and cradled Rhys's face, his fingers biting into Rhys's skin. "In all the years we've known each other, I never truly knew you. The real you. The man whose smile can take me higher than I've ever flown." Wade inhaled shakily when tears suddenly pooled in Rhys's shocked eyes and overspilled onto his cheeks. He wiped at the wetness on Rhys's heated skin with his thumbs. "And whose tears can bring me lower than I've ever fallen. The man who I've chased after for most of my professional life, competing for the same contracts, always seeking his attention, always searching for his approval." A low chuckle left Wade's lips. "*Shit*, even going as far as to coerce him into going into business with me."

"What are you saying?" Rhys whispered brokenly, the fresh tears welling in his eyes causing Wade's heart to twist in agony.

"I'm saying that it kills me that we've been so close yet so far this past sixteen years," Wade said tremulously, lowering his head to kiss the damp trails on Rhys's cheeks. "It kills me that you slept with all those men when you could have been sleeping with me. It kills me that I broke your heart every single time

I went off with a woman." He took a deep breath and gazed hotly into Rhys's stunned eyes. "Because I love you, Rhys. It doesn't matter that you're a man. My soul chose you a long time ago. It's taken sixteen years for my body and my heart to catch up."

A sob tore out of Rhys's lips. He clutched Wade's sweater and dropped his forehead on Wade's chest, his body trembling violently against Wade's.

"So don't give up on us, Rhys," Wade said, his lips on Rhys's hair while he wrapped his arms around Rhys's body. "Fight for this. Fight *with* me. Fight for *us*. God help me, I will spend the rest of my life making up for our lost time if you would only say yes to me. Tell me, Rhys. Tell me yes. Tell me that you love me too."

Rhys's knuckles whitened in the material of Wade's sweater. He took a shuddering breath before slowly raising his chin and staring up at Wade.

Wade's heart constricted at the light blazing in Rhys's eyes.

"Yes," Rhys breathed, emotion painting red flags on his cheekbones.

Wade pressed his lips to Rhys's in a featherlight touch. "I want to hear it, Rhys."

Rhys shuddered and lifted his hands to the back of Wade's head. "I love you," he said fervently. "I've always loved you. And I always will. Until the day I die."

Wade closed his eyes for a moment, emotion clogging his throat while wetness stung the back of his eyelids, his heart overflowing with his feelings for Rhys.

Then he took Rhys's lips with his mouth, pouring

everything he was and everything he wanted them to be into the torrid kiss.

Rhys moaned and opened up for him, his fingers curling in Wade's hair, his body heating up in Wade's arms.

Desire filled Wade, a yearning so strong it brought a groan of pure need up his throat. He leaned down, grabbed the back of Rhys's thighs, and lifted him up against his body. Rhys whimpered against Wade's lips, his long legs wrapping instinctively around Wade's waist while his arms closed on Wade's shoulders.

"The bedroom?" Wade grunted, nipping at Rhys's lips.

"Down that corridor," Rhys murmured shakily, indicating a passage leading off the far end of the lounge.

Wade turned and headed in that direction with Rhys in his arms, passion a growing blaze inside his chest. In that instant, Wade knew he needed more than just sex with Rhys tonight.

He wanted a declaration. An affirmation. A promise.

The beginning of them.

I can feel his lips. His kiss. His touch. The weight of his body on me. The lustful look in his eyes. His heat as he enters me. His strength as he takes me. His heavy breaths as he thrusts into my body.

Even in my filthiest fantasies, Wade was never like this.

So rough. So demanding. So hungry. He drags me along by brute force, his giant body pinning me down to the bed while he impales me. My field of vision narrows. My reasoning is wrecked. I get muddled.

I want more.

❧

THE WAY RHYS TAKES ME TO THE HILT, DEEP IN HIS ASS. HIS moans and his shivers as he rides me. His gasps and the way he trembles when I turn him on his front and do him doggy style. I feel like I'm going out of my mind. I have never been filled with such desire before. The desire to take. To brand. To tame. To see him submit to me. But also to cherish. To protect. To revere.

This is more than I thought I ever wanted. So much more. And I need it all so badly I can taste him on my tongue. Yearn for him so badly that I wish this moment would never end. One thing I'm certain of.

I will never let him go.

He is my world. And I am his gravity.

EPILOGUE

RHYS STIRRED AND SIGHED, HIS MUSCLES ACHING pleasantly as he stretched his legs. The man holding him against his chest brushed his lips across Rhys's forehead.

"'Morning," Wade murmured.

"Hmm," Rhys hummed. "'Morning." He blinked his eyes open and looked fuzzily at Wade. "What time is it?"

Wade smiled, his gaze full of warmth. "I love how untamed your hair is in the morning." He nuzzled the unruly blond locks on Rhys's head. "Makes me want to mess it up even more. And it's—," he picked his watch off the nightstand and glanced at the dial, "—three in the afternoon."

Rhys rose up slightly and looked over his shoulder at the glass wall opposite the bed, heat from the flames burning in the fireplace licking faintly over his bare skin. Snow painted the forest and mountains outside in a breathtaking sea of white under cloudless blue skies.

"It's Christmas," Rhys mumbled.

"Uh-huh," Wade said, his lips finding Rhys's throat.

Rhys shivered and arched his neck, giving Wade better access. "I can't believe we fucked for two days straight."

"I love it when you talk dirty," Wade drawled, his hands sliding sensuously down Rhys's back to cup his ass. "And, I gotta admit, two days is my personal best to date."

Rhys groaned and clutched Wade's shoulders. He'd lost count of the number of times Wade had said "love" since the night he turned up at the cabin and stormed his way past all of Rhys's defenses to capture his heart once more.

To say that Wade's confession had shocked Rhys to the core and nearly robbed him of his senses would be a gross understatement. Never in a million years could he have imagined that Wade had felt something for him all along. Something he hadn't been able to define for all those years, until the night he witnessed Rhys making love to himself while shouting out Wade's name.

Wade's incredible admission and what had happened between them afterward were forever etched in Rhys's mind, memories he would cherish for the rest of their lives and take to his grave.

Rhys's dick stirred as Wade slipped his fingers in the crack of Rhys's butt and ran his thumb over the pucker of his hole, his teeth nipping at Rhys's skin, adding to the marks he had already made.

Rhys moaned when he felt Wade's erection dig

persistently into his belly. Though he was a little sore after the sex fest of the past two days, Rhys knew he would be unable to deny Wade. And he didn't want to.

He rose up on his hands, kissed Wade passionately, and slid his way down Wade's body until his mouth found Wade's thick, hot cock.

Wade shuddered and groaned, his fingers curling in Rhys's hair, messing it up further.

TEN DAYS LATER

GABE BLINKED SLOWLY, HIS EXPRESSION STUNNED AS HE stared from Rhys to Wade and back again.

"What?" he mumbled.

Wade smiled. "We want you to become a partner in Damon & Tucker." He glanced at Rhys where the latter stood beside his chair. "It's something we've had in mind for a while. And we think now is the right time to bring you on board."

Gabe's knuckles whitened where he'd unconsciously gripped the armrests of his seat. He swallowed.

"Are you sure?"

"Yes," Rhys said with a grin. "Of course, if you don't want it—" he added in a teasing tone.

"I want it!" Gabe said in a rush. He colored slightly under Wade and Rhys's amused gazes. "I mean, yes."

It was the first week of January and the office was

buzzing with activity once more. They were scheduled to complete the Osaka contract in five days, and Gabe's long-term project in Hawaii was also coming to a close. In addition to their forthcoming proposal with the president of Keele Industries, they'd been approached by the CEO of Rutherford Industries and the young heir to the Colby Corporation for a rather special project in the Pacific Ocean.

Although Wade was excited at the way their business was thriving, he was a hundred times more thrilled about finally possessing the man standing next to him body, heart, and soul. They'd ended up spending a week at the cabin in the mountains and reluctantly returned to Tokyo on New Year's Eve. Wade had contacted Joe and Ethan on Christmas Day and updated them on how things had gone in Nagano, while Rhys spoke to Michael and thanked him.

It had taken all of Wade's patience since they'd returned to the city not to scream from the top of his lungs and announce to the whole wide world that Rhys Damon belonged to him.

Wade suspected Rhys wouldn't mind if he made their relationship public, but he wanted the two of them to talk about it first and decide how they would announce it to their wider circle of friends and their employees. Wade suspected most would be shocked and hoped the majority would be happy for them.

Not that it mattered at the end of the day.

Wade knew what he wanted and what he wanted was Rhys. And as long as Rhys was his, he didn't much care what the rest of the world thought of him.

They had their first opportunity to reveal the change in their relationship that very evening, when they went to *Saron* for a drink. To Wade's surprise, there were two women seated at the bar. One of them was Lana Keele. Perched on a barstool next to her was Eveline Claude, the owner of *Le Secret* and one of their clients.

"Hey Rhys, long time no see," Eveline said, flashing them a smile. She cocked an eyebrow at Wade. "I didn't know this was one of your watering holes too."

"Wade?" Lana said, surprise widening her green eyes as she leaned around the blonde and stared at Wade.

"Hi, Lana," Wade said. He glanced at Rhys's curious expression and made the introductions while they settled on a pair of barstools. "Lana, this is my partner, Rhys Damon. Rhys, Lana Keele."

Rhys smiled and shook Lana's hand, his gaze bereft of accusation as he studied the brunette who had almost ended their relationship. Wade could tell Rhys had noted that Wade hadn't used the words "business partner".

"I know we have a meeting set up this Friday, but it's nice to finally meet you," Rhys told Lana.

"It's nice to meet you too," Lana said amiably, her cheeks dimpling as she grinned. She glanced between Rhys and Wade. "I must say, working with you two is going to keep me, er, hot under the collar."

Wade suppressed a chuckle at Rhys's startled expression.

"I kinda see what you mean, now," Rhys murmured drily.

"What?" Lana said, her cat-like eyes glinting with curiosity. "Did Wade say something about me?"

"One minute," someone stated stonily behind them. "I was gone one goddamn minute and you're already flirting with someone."

Wade twisted on his seat and nodded a greeting at Tom Sutherland where the latter stood staring grouchily at Lana.

"What I do in my free time is none of your business," Lana bristled while Eveline giggled. "And why are you here again?"

"To keep an eye on you. I know what you're like when you've had one too many," Tom retorted. "Besides, nothing strikes more fear in an assistant's heart than hearing the words *I'm going to go out and get royally fucked tonight* out of the mouth of his boss when he knows she's got a business meeting at seven a.m. the following morning." He looked around at the busy crowd filling the club. "If I knew you were coming here, I would have spent the night catching up on tomorrow's proposal."

Rhys leaned close to Wade. "Ah. I see what you meant by *that,* too," he whispered, amused.

Wade had to quell the sudden urge to kiss Rhys as Rhys's scent tickled his nostrils.

A private door opened next to the back of the bar. Joe and Ethan appeared, heads close as they spoke to each other in low voices, their arms grazing intimately.

Eveline took one look at their slightly disheveled

clothes and the color on Ethan's cheeks before heaving a sigh.

"Seriously, you two need to stop screwing like rabbits every damn chance you get and rubbing your hot sex life in your single friends' faces," she said, pursing her lips. "It's darn irritating."

"You're just jealous 'cause you're not getting any," Ethan said blithely while Joe grinned and dropped a kiss on his head.

"Well, I can't deny that the thickest thing my vajayjay has seen of late is a dildo," Eveline admitted with a grimace.

Rhys twitched on the stool next to Wade. Wade eyed Rhys's reddening ears and bit back a smile as he recalled the sinful play they'd had with Rhys's sex toy two nights ago.

"Wade?" someone said behind them.

Wade looked over his shoulder and saw Gabe and his fiancé Cam Sorvino appear through the crowd.

"Hey, Gabe," Wade said. He turned and shook Cam's hand. "Cam, it's great to see you again."

"It's good to see you too, Wade," Cam said with a nod and a smile.

Rhys glanced between Gabe and Cam before cocking an eyebrow at Gabe. "You told him yet?"

Cam grinned and took Gabe's hand in his own. "Yes, he did. That's why we're here tonight. To celebrate."

"Oh," Ethan said curiously. "What are we celebrating?"

Cam gazed at the blushing man beside him. "Gabe

just made partner," he said, pride underscoring his voice.

"Oh wow!" Lana blinked as warm congratulations echoed along the counter, Ethan leaning over to hug Gabe and slap him on the back. "So, I get to work with *three* hotties?" She fanned herself, her eyes twinkling with amusement.

Tom groaned beside her. "Well, considering they're all batting for the other team, I think I can safely say you're not going to get in their pants."

Lana's eyes widened as she gazed at her secretary. "Huh? What do you mean?"

Eveline stared from Rhys to Wade, awareness dawning in her gaze. "Oh."

Tom grunted. "My spidey sense has yet to let me down when it comes to these things."

Gabe opened and closed his mouth soundlessly as Tom's meaning finally sank in. "Come again?" he finally stammered, blue eyes wide with shock.

※

RHYS SIGHED AT THE STUNNED EXPRESSIONS AROUND them.

Though he didn't mind their friends knowing about his and Wade's relationship, he would have preferred if Wade and him had announced it on their own terms.

Looks like that's not going to happen now.

Rhys startled when Wade suddenly took his hand.

Wade gazed at him hotly. "I'm not batting for a team. I only bat for one man," he said to the others. He dropped a kiss on the back of Rhys's knuckles and grinned when Rhys flushed. "And yes, Gabe. I have come. Many times."

Rhys groaned and covered his face with his other hand. *I can't believe he just said that.*

Ethan chuckled from the other side of the counter. "Way to broadcast your status as a couple, you guys. Now we won't have to tiptoe around you two and watch every damn word that comes out of our mouths when our common acquaintances are within earshot."

Eveline brightened. "Oh, so Wade knows about Joe and Rhys being fuck buddies in New York?"

Rhys stiffened on the barstool beside Wade.

"*Ah-ha!*" Ethan stared smugly at Joe. "So I was right."

Lana propped her elbows on the counter and cupped her chin in her hands, her avid green gaze shifting from Wade, to Rhys and Joe, and back again.

Eveline flashed Joe and Rhys a nervous smile. "Er, was that still meant to be a secret?"

"Kinda," Joe muttered. "It wasn't really up to me to disclose it." He sighed at Ethan's self-satisfied expression. "I thought you'd be more pissed off."

Ethan shrugged. "I can't deny that it irks me a bit, but that has more to do with you not telling me the truth than it does with the fact itself."

Rhys turned to face Wade, his eyes full of wary determination. "I—"

Wade leaned in and kissed him while their friends started teasing Eveline for not being able to keep a secret. "As long as I'm the only one you fuck from now on, I don't really care," he murmured against Rhys's lips.

Rhys blinked, surprised. "Hmm, okay."

"I *am* the only one you're going to fuck from now on, right, Rhys?" Wade teased, running his hands up from Rhys's knees to Rhys's thighs.

"Uh-huh," Rhys mumbled, his eyes glazing over at Wade's touch.

Wade leaned toward him and pressed his forehead against Rhys's. "I'm so head over heels in love with you," he murmured.

Rhys swallowed, overcome with emotion. *I'm going to die from happiness.*

Wade's expression slowly sobered as his slate-blue eyes drilled steadily into Rhys's. "I've been thinking about something." He hesitated before glancing down and gently stroking Rhys's ring finger. "How would you feel if one day I want to show the world that you belong to me in the most irrevocable way one person can belong to another?"

Rhys inhaled sharply. He stared at Wade, stunned at how easily words of love and adoration fell from his lips and the meaning behind his question.

"I would be honored," Rhys replied, blinking back sudden tears. He bit his lip. "Are you—are you sure?"

"Absolutely, positively, one hundred percent sure," Wade said, pressing his lips softly to Rhys's.

"Only one hundred?" Rhys teased, his heart full to bursting.

Wade smiled. "A thousand percent."

Rhys arched an eyebrow.

"A million percent." Wade grinned and took Rhys's mouth in a searing kiss full of promise.

THE END

What happens when a sexy club owner meets her hot, new business rival?

Get Undisclosed (Nights #7)
Turn the page to read an extract now!

UNDISCLOSED (NIGHTS SERIES BOOK 7) SPECIAL PREVIEW

Eveline Claude blinked slowly. "Come again?"

A muscle jumped in the jawline of the man seated on the other side of the conference room table.

"You don't own the freehold to the Tokyo branch of *Le Secret*," Malcolm Brooks repeated stiffly.

Eveline's pulse started to race as she stared from Brooks to his poker-faced partner, Victor Kline.

"I'm sorry, did I just hear you say that I don't own the tenure of one of my most successful business enterprises?" Silence greeted her stunned question. "Are you guys yanking my chain right now?" Eveline chuckled in disbelief. "You are, aren't you? Because there's no way my one-thousand-dollar-per-hour, top-notch city lawyers just informed me that they fucked up."

Brooks glanced at Kline. "Told you she'd bring up the hourly fee," he muttered.

Kline ignored his partner and studied Eveline with

an impassive expression. "Of course, we'll be working to resolve this matter pro bono. The mistake is ours and we cannot apologize enough on behalf of the firm."

Eveline's mouth went dry as she looked between the two men and realized they were serious. The first inkling that her day was going to turn out to be gloriously shitty began at six a.m., when the fire alarm in her apartment building went off. Having left *Le Secret* at two, Eveline wasn't pleased that her much needed beauty sleep had been interrupted by some asshole who hadn't figured out how to use his new waffle maker. Her ire rose tenfold when she went to collect her car from the underground garage and noticed the fresh scratch on her midnight blue Maserati. She'd made a note to ask the security guards to check the cameras covering the parking lot and had barreled out of the building and into the early morning Tokyo traffic at twice the allowed speed limit; she hated being late for an appointment and her nine o'clock meeting with Brooks & Kline was taking place on the other side of town. She'd made it to their office on the twelfth floor of the glass and steel high-rise housing their law firm with four minutes to spare and had waited impatiently in the conference room, curious as to why they'd requested the urgent face to face.

It was Brooks who'd called her the day before to set up the meeting.

"Something's come up. We need to talk," the lawyer said cryptically after Eveline's assistant put his call through.

Eveline paused and lowered her cup of coffee, her gaze shifting from the busy dual computer screens on the desk before her, to the glorious views beyond the panoramic windows to her right. Her office was located next to a small, private flat she kept above Le Secret and overlooked Ginza, the most famous and exclusive district in Tokyo.

Eveline frowned as she studied the busy intersection outside, the first seed of unease stirring inside her.

"What's this about, Malcolm? It's rare for you to call me yourself."

"I know. It would be best if we had this conversation face to face," Brooks replied.

He'd refused to answer Eveline's questions and gave her the details of their appointment before disconnecting. Though she'd been troubled by her enigmatic conversation with the lawyer, Eveline soon forgot about the exchange, the daily demands of running her internationally renowned and incredibly successful chain of upscale escort clubs consuming all her attention and focus. Business was booming, especially since she'd opened the latest branch of *Le Secret* in Singapore.

Eveline swallowed presently and leaned back in the sleek metal and leather chair of the conference room, her knuckles whitening where she gripped the arm rests. *Maybe I should have thrown salt over my left shoulder before I left my apartment this morning. Or burned some incense or do whatever it is people do to ward off bad luck.*

She studied the two lawyers with narrowed eyes. "Explain to me exactly how this happened."

Brooks sighed and pinched the bridge of his nose while Kline slid a file across the table.

"It seems Mr. Nagato forged the documents his lawyers provided to us five years ago, when he sold you the plot in Ginza as a freehold," Brooks said bitterly. "What you actually bought off him was the right to lease. His son-in-law works for the local land registry office and we suspect he made the counterfeit papers. According to one of our contacts in the Tokyo Metropolitan Police Department, the Nagatos have connections with an organized crime syndicate that specializes in land rights grabs."

Eveline tensed, her gaze skimming the folder before her distractedly. "You mean, they're part of the Yakuza?"

Kline grimaced. "They are linked to them in a distant, convoluted fashion, yes."

Eveline's heart pounded as she digested the implication of the lawyers' words. The Yakuza were the Japanese equivalent of the Italian Mafia. Having witnessed secondhand what the mob did to their business rivals in New York, Eveline had no desire to associate with the local criminal organizations here in Japan, even if she suspected several of the clients who had visited the Tokyo branch of *Le Secret* over the last five years had some kind of connection to them.

Eveline clenched her jaw. "What can we do about this? I paid Nagato a hefty sum of money for that land. We're talking seven figures here, as you both well know." She paused, an unwelcome thought bringing a bitter taste to her mouth. "Wait. Did he even *own* that plot? Don't tell me the asshole sold me someone else's—"

"He does," Kline said. "Or he did."

"We've already lodged an appeal in court to contest the new owner's claim to the freehold," Brooks said. He ran a hand through his hair. "It's going to take some time to—"

"New owner?" Eveline scowled. "What the hell do you mean, *new owner?*" She jumped to her feet and leaned her hands on the table. "Are you telling me that conniving bastard sold *my* land to someone else?!"

"Yes," Brooks said quietly. "And this time, the documents he provided were the legitimate ones."

Eveline took a shuddering breath and closed her eyes briefly, her nails biting into her palms where she'd fisted her fingers.

"I'm gonna kill him," she hissed. Eveline grabbed her bag and stormed toward the conference room exit. "I'm gonna strangle that lowlife with my bare hands and dump his body in Tokyo Bay! What's his address?"

"Sit down, Eveline," Kline said with a sigh.

Eveline stopped by the door and whirled around. "I'm not kidding, Victor! I hope you guys know a good criminal lawyer 'cause I'm going to need—"

"Nagato is dead," Brooks said.

Eveline froze. She opened and closed her mouth soundlessly, her eyes rounding as she gaped at the two lawyers.

"*What?!*" she shrieked.

"Nagato died three weeks ago," Kline stated. "It was a heart attack, apparently."

A light-headed feeling swept over Eveline. She made her way back to the table on unsteady legs and flopped down in the chair she had just vacated.

"He completed the sale of the freehold a few days before his death," Brooks added.

Kline leaned across the table and opened the file in front of Eveline. "This is the letter we received yesterday from the new owner's law firm."

Eveline blinked before focusing on the top sheet of the paperwork before her.

"The land in Ginza is now the property of Lincoln Hudson, the President and CEO of the Hudson Group," Kline continued. "His lawyers have given us formal notice that *Le Secret*'s leasehold rights will be revoked in thirty days."

Eveline's hands trembled as she picked up the letter and read it over, the words blurring in front of her eyes. Her heart sank as she finally absorbed its content.

It was just as Kline had said.

The new owner of the plot on which *Le Secret* stood had given her thirty days to dissolve her business and vacate his land.

"Wouldn't a leasehold be for fifty years?" Eveline mumbled. "Can he even do this?"

"The new leasehold law that came into effect twenty-five years ago gives the landowner the right to refuse the leaseholder permission to run a business on his property," Kline said. "Hudson is completely within his rights to issue a revocation order."

Blood thundered in Eveline's ears, the sound matching the emotions storming through her as she stared blindly at the printed text. She put the letter down, inhaled shakily, and stared at the men opposite her.

When it rains, it fucking pours.

"How long will the court appeal take?" she said, her voice growing steely as cogwheels started turning in her brain. She had not come this far in life without learning how to roll with some punches. Eveline frowned. *Or how to get back up and knock the enemy right out of the ring.*

"Six weeks," Brooks said.

Eveline drummed the fingers of her right hand on the table, her polished, red-lacquered nails rapping an impatient tempo.

"Can we do anything to expedite it?"

"We've got a meeting with one of the judges this afternoon," Kline said. "As to whether he will be willing to bring the case forward is not something I'd want to bet money on."

Eveline gritted her teeth. "Do the Hudson Group President and his lawyers know the details of this affair? As in Nagato swindling me out of—"

"They know," Brooks said. "We spoke to Lincoln Hudson's lawyers and his secretary yesterday after we received the letter. Hudson's secretary got back to us thirty minutes ago."

Eveline leaned forward in her chair, her heart pounding against her ribs. "And? Is he willing to negotiate something?"

"Hudson said that it ain't his problem," Kline muttered.

Eveline stilled. "What?"

Brooks rubbed his eyes tiredly. "According to his secretary, Lincoln Hudson's exact words were 'I don't give a flying fuck'."

Read Undisclosed today

AFTERWORD

To all my friends who helped make this possible. You know who you are.

To you, my readers. Thank you for reading Rhys and Wade's electrifying love story. I hope you loved this sixth book in the Nights series. I would be grateful if you could leave a review on Goodreads or on the store where you purchased this book. Reviews help readers like you find my books and I truly appreciate your honest opinions about my stories.

Make sure to sign up to my store newsletter for special deals on my books and new release alerts. Or you can sign up to my author newsletter instead to get upcoming release notifications, sneak peeks, and giveaways.

ABOUT THE AUTHOR

Ava Marie Salinger is the romance pen name of an Amazon bestselling author with a passion for writing addictive tales. Known for her action-packed and thrilling urban fantasy novels, she has expanded her repertoire with the introduction of the M/M urban fantasy romance series Fallen Messengers. Additionally, she has penned the scorching hot contemporary M/M romance series Nights and Twilight Falls as A.M. Salinger. When not immersed in her writing, Ava can be found curating inspiring music playlists, indulging in her love for nature, marveling at the latest gadgets, and savoring Chinese cuisine.

You can find all of Ava's books on her author store at shop.adstarrling.com